Advance Praise for *Fun*

"...Shipp's writing is alarmingly bizarre, but th[e] consciousness that is woven throughout these stories. [Every tale has its] own world, its own universe in a nutshell, and yet they are linked by Shipp's increasingly sophisticated insights on what it means to be human. This book is a triumph."
—Joe McKinney, *Quarantined* and *Apocalypse of the Dead*

"The stories contained in this volume are extremely original, compelling, chaotic, twisted, and undeniable. This is truly imagination unleashed."—*Morpheus Tales*

"Each story was unique and the prose is so well done, the words perfectly manipulated to flow almost like poetry. I was incredibly impressed that such disjointed images could be captured and relayed so well, through the written word."—*ReadReviewer*

"[Shipp] has an uncanny ability to reach you through a story, grab you by the neck and shake you until your eyeballs twitch. And this isn't as bad as it sounds; no, he makes you want to read more, and makes me want to live one of his stories."—Keith Dugger

"As I was reading this collection, I kept trying to decide whether Jeremy Shipp's skull was really a giant blender filled with lysergic acid and pixie dust—topped off with a healthy dose of aged absinthe—or a spooky insane asylum peopled with creepy attic clowns, mischievous goblins, gnomes, tree spirits, zombie polar bears, and other assorted freaks."—*Ye Olde Imagination Shoppe*

"At every turn in these stories, Shipp demonstrates a macabre whimsy."
—*Dust & Corruption*

"You're in for a something surreal, something beautifully fantastic and I promise you, you won't be bothered by the battle scars you walk away with. You'll be grateful, satisfied that you bear those marks, proud that you took the journey right along with these misguided, damaged characters."—TS Tate

"This is a truly excellent selection of short stories from perhaps the most sensitive member of the modern Bizarro literary scene. His stories manage to be both weird and heartfelt."—T.J. McIntyre

"...Shipp manages to find meaning and soul in the craziest of stories. This bizarro collection will leave you laughing, crying, and hiding under the covers. Sometimes all at once."—Daniel Pyle, *Dismember* and *Down the Drain*

"...dark and edgy, blurring the line between fantasy and reality with ease. Jeremy C. Shipp delves deep into the human psyche to reveal man's worst fears."
—Amy Grech, *Blanket of White* and *Fallen Angel*

Acknowledgements

"Just Another Vampire Story" first published in *Darkness Rising 2: Hideous Dreams*
"Ticketyboo" first published in *Flesh & Blood Magazine*
"The Escapist" first published in *Horror World*
"Monkey Boy and the Monsters" first published in *Mosaic Art and Literary Journal*
"Kingdom Come" first published in *Harlan County Horrors*

Fungus of the Heart © 2010
by Jeremy C. Shipp

Published by Raw Dog Screaming Press
Bowie, MD

First Edition

Cover design: M. Garrow Bourke
Book design: Jennifer Barnes

Printed in the United States of America

ISBN: 978-1-935738-01-5

Library of Congress Control Number: 2010933091

www.RawDogScreaming.com

Fungus
of the
Heart

collected fiction

Jeremy C. Shipp

RAW DOG SCREAMING PRESS

Also by Jeremy C. Shipp

Novels

Vacation

Cursed

Collected Fiction

Sheep and Wolves

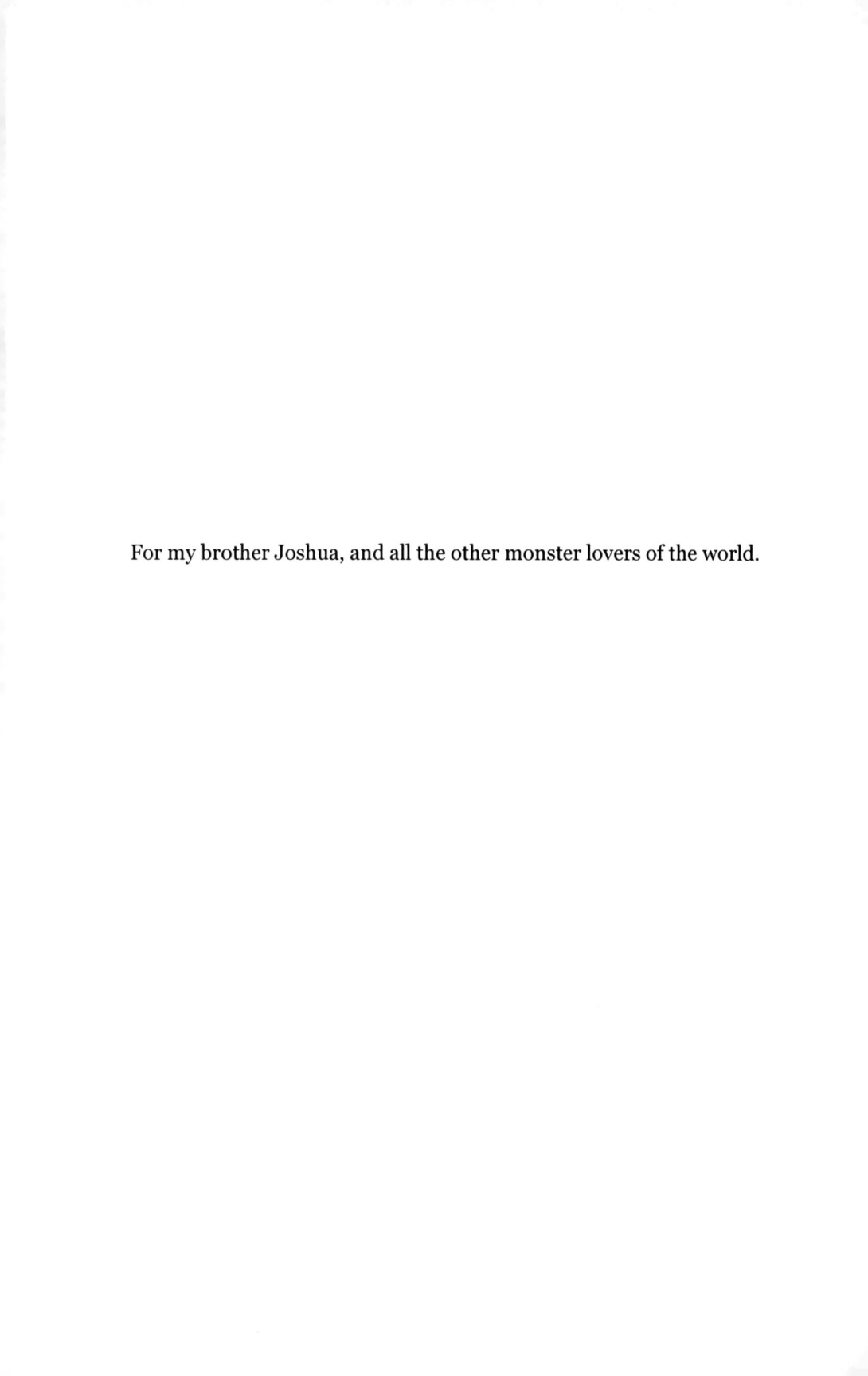

For my brother Joshua, and all the other monster lovers of the world.

Table of Contents

The Sun Never Rises in the Big City 9

The Haunted House 29

Fungus of the Heart 41

Boy in the Cabinet 67

Just Another Vampire Story 79

Ticketyboo 83

The Escapist 93

Ula Morales 107

Spider House 111

Monkey Boy and the Monsters 117

Agape Walrus 129

Kingdom Come 137

How to Make a Clown 153

The Sun Never Rises in the Big City

Adeline positions herself in front of the Venetian blinds, and the blades of light cut her body into thin slices. As expected, she's wearing the black dress I bought her for my thirty-fifth birthday. And I can tell she's been working on her game face.

I smile. "How can I help you, Adeline?"

"That depends, Mr. Edge," she says. "How do you feel about pro bono work?"

"I can't afford to be nice."

"What about for old friends?"

"You're not my friend."

Adeline laughs a little, then holds out her cigarette. "Surely you're generous enough to share your fire."

I hold a lit match close to her face. And this has nothing to do with nice.

"Thanks," she says, taking the rod into her mouth, sucking in the poison.

This time, she doesn't cough.

I almost thank her.

After a few more toxic breaths, she takes an envelope out of her purse. "One thousand now. I'll pay the rest when you get the job done."

I count the money. "Alright. So who's the unlucky bastard this time?"

"My husband."

"I thought he was killed in combat."

"So did I. So did everyone. Turns out he was the only one who survived the bombing. A local farmer took him to his house, and Marty lived with the enemy for the next six months. He didn't know any better."

"Post-traumatic amnesia?"

"Right. Eventually, his memories returned, and he killed the family, and came home."

"So what's the problem? The war change him?"

"No, Marty's the same asshole he always was. I'm the one who's changed. I'm not the naïve country belle he married, and I can tell when someone's cheating on me. It's one thing for a soldier to relieve himself with barbarian whores while he's thousands of miles from his wife. But he's home now. And I should be more than enough woman for him."

"You should sound angrier."

"Sorry."

"Don't say sorry. Just keep going."

Adeline nods. "And I should be more than enough woman for him."

"You are. You're too much woman for any man."

"Are you making fun of me, Mr. Edge?"

"I wouldn't dream of it."

Adeline gives a look like she's ready to wring my neck. Then she laughs. "So what do you say? Will you be my private dick again?"

"You don't need me for this, Adeline. You're more than capable of catching Marty in the act."

"True, but when that time comes, I'll need you there to keep me from killing him."

"Alright."

"One more thing. I won't be able to pay you the rest of your money until three months from now."

"You said you'd pay me when I get the job done."

Adeline stands, and leans against my desk, her cleavage spilling towards me. "Please, Frank. I don't want to do this by myself."

And maybe my friends are right. Maybe I'm sick in the head, and I enjoy succumbing to a woman's charms.

But it's not as if I'm really powerless.

I could snap my fingers, and she'd show me more than this small portion of her breasts. I could reach into my desk, press the button, and she'd lose everything.

So maybe I am crazy.

But I'm still a man.

The problem with stakeouts is that Adeline hates spending long periods of time in enclosed spaces, and her anxieties usually end up ruining the mood. But tonight, she's really on top of her game.

She hasn't even stuttered once.

"This is a bad idea," I say.

Adeline wipes the sweat off her forehead. "You only say that because you didn't come up with it."

"You two may be identical, but Berta's nothing like you. Marty will see through her."

"Berta knows what she's doing. If you recall, my sister's a professional actor."

"That's debatable. I've been to one of her shows."

"She'll be fine. Marty and I don't talk much, so all Berta has to do is sit there and look pretty. And that's something the women in my family are very good at."

"True enough."

Adeline smiles. "Is that your sly way of paying me a compliment, Mr. Edge?"

"Keep dreaming, sweetheart."

"I will." She pulls up my sleeve, and checks my watch. "Marty should be leaving for one of his so-called business meetings soon. He's a devil behind the wheel, so you'll have to break the law to keep up with him."

"I know how to do my job."

At this point, Adeline gasps, and coughs, and gasps again.

"Adeline?" I say.

"No!" she says, clawing at my face with both hands.

I pinch her arm.

She hugs her chest, and glares at me. "Fuck you, Frank. I did everything you wanted me to do. Every fucking thing."

"I didn't do this," I say. "I didn't even bring the Remote with me."

"You're an asshole. I wish—" She gasps again, and stops talking.

I check for a pulse.

And probably due to the shock of the situation, my defenses weaken, and I almost cry.

"Adeline," I say. "Maria."

I stare at her lifeless body until the front door of the mansion opens. Then a dark figure approaches my car. So I roll down my window.

"Dinner's ready," Margaret says, smiling at me. And like any good wife, she ignores Adeline completely.

"Alright," I say. "I'll be right in."

"Do you want me to wait for you?"

"No. Go on ahead."

My wife's a pro at hiding her feelings, but tonight I can detect her anxiety. Because she giggles all the way back to the house.

Her doctor has her on a strict laugh regimen in order to lower her stress levels and strengthen her immune system. She needs to be healthy and strong, because I want another boy.

I decide to deal with Adeline's body later.

So I take off my fedora and trench coat.

And kiss her corpse goodbye.

Sex with Margaret normally jostles my frustrations and forces them from my mind, but this morning is anything but normal. And I can't stop thinking about Adeline.

I don't know who killed her, and I don't know who stole her body from my car last night.

But the real mystery is why I even give a damn.

Adeline was a rag, after all. Human, though just barely.

No one in their right mind would spend any time or energy over such a pathetic loss.

So I really must be crazy.

After filling my wife with my legacy, I get out of bed, and put on my pants. "I'm going to the office."

"OK," my wife says.

I don't kiss her goodbye, because she didn't make me forget my problems.

Margaret laughs.

A short drive later, I'm in my office, and the Remote isn't in the bottom drawer of my desk.

So I search the entire room.

Nothing.

More often than not, when a Remote goes missing, the culprit's usually the rag bound to the device. But I strongly doubt Adeline killed herself.

She worked too hard to please me.

To survive.

My gut tells me Adeline's death was a murder, and I can almost feel the murderer's presence. I'm sure he's still out there.

Lurking in the shadows of this labyrinth we call a city.

And if I don't do something, he'll get away with the killing.

Fungus of the Heart

I could hire a private investigator, but I'm sure he'd wonder why I'd spend so much money investigating the death of a rag. He'd look down on me, so that's out of the question.

I can't call the police either, because they'd just laugh at me. Legally, killing a rag isn't murder. And according to the handbook, in the case of a rag's death, we're supposed to call up the Agency and ask for a replacement.

Because people are cheap. Investigations aren't.

So if I want to find this killer, I'm gonna have to do the legwork myself.

"You're an idiot, Frank," I say.

And I call up the Agency, enter my ID number, and wait.

Finally, a man says, "How can we help you, sire?"

"My Remote's missing," I say.

"Would you like your replacement sent to your home address?"

"That won't be necessary. I just want the coordinates."

"We'll transmit them to your handheld in ten to fifteen minutes. Do you need the coordinates for your rag as well?"

"She's dead."

"We're sorry for the inconvenience. Would you like your replacement sent to your home address?"

"I don't want a replacement. Not yet."

"If you were dissatisfied with your previous rag, we'd be happy to send you a new questionnaire. We can assure you—"

"I wasn't unhappy with her. I didn't kill her. I'm just too busy for a new rag right now. I'll call you back when I want a new one."

"Thank you, sire. Is there anything else we can do for you today?"

"No."

I hang up.

About half an hour later, I'm standing in an alley, in front of an adobe dome.

I check my handheld again.

This is the right place.

Since there's no door, I say, "Hello?"

Moments later, a man wearing a neon tunic climbs out of a hole in the top of the dome. He sits up there, and aims a slingshot at me. "Can I help you?"

I pull my mag out, and point the barrel at his face. "Put the toy down."

"I'd rather not."

"If you hit me with that thing, I won't hesitate to kill you."

"I won't shoot you unless you attack me."

"What if your fingers slip?"

"That doesn't usually happen."

"Did you steal my Remote?"

The neon man lowers his slingshot. "Oh, you're him. I'll be right back." He disappears down the hole.

I wait for over five minutes. "Are you hiding in there?"

Finally, the man returns with the Remote. My Remote. "Sorry that took me so long. I forgot where I put it."

I point the gun at him again. "Give it to me."

He obeys, throwing the Remote at me.

And I catch the device with my free hand, and say, "Why'd you kill her?"

He laughs. "I didn't kill anyone. I'm a Nymph."

So he's one of those pacifistic sissies out to ruin this great country.

My finger twitches, and I almost pull the trigger. Because I remember the day I found one of those Nymph pamphlets in my thirteen-year-old's closet. Thankfully, I made this discovery in time. I sent my son to boot camp the next day, and when he returned six months later, he was good as new.

Still, these bastards nearly emasculated my son with ideological poison. And that's not something I can forgive.

"A man gave me the Remote," the Nymph says.

I take a deep breath, and lower my weapon. "What man?"

"I don't know. He didn't tell me his name."

"What did he look like?"

"He was wearing a mask. Like a gorilla. He told me you'd be coming for the Remote eventually. He said I should give you a message. Something about a clock, I think. To be honest, I was halfway in another plane at the time. But I definitely remember him mentioning a clock."

"That's all you can tell me?"

"Yeah."

So I pull the trigger.

I miss, and he ducks into his hole. Then I blast his dome a few times, and the pansy shouts something about Gaia's heart.

Maybe I hit him. Maybe I didn't.

Either way, no one's going to try to kill me for this. The only people who care about Nymphs are other Nymphs, and they're certainly not going to seek vengeance. They're pathetic.

And if I killed this coward, then I did him a favor.

"You're welcome," I say.

In the bunkhouse, my servants take turns holding my balls, testifying to their innocence. And they know I won't hesitate to exercise my legal right to blow their brains out if I catch them in a lie. So I watch their eyes.

Victor the cook says, "I didn't kill her, sire. I would never vandalize your property."

And Victor looks anxious, suspicious, guilty.

The only problem is, so did everyone else.

"You're lying," I say. "If you tell me the truth now, I'll let you live."

"I don't know anything," Victor says.

"I know you know something. Your friends told me. They sold you out."

"They're liars."

I point my mag at his face. "You're the liar."

Then Victor releases my testicles, and cries into his hands.

"Put those back," I say.

The cook obeys. "I'm sorry, sire. I stole her body. Please don't kill me."

I lower the gun. "Did you kill her?"

"No."

"Where's the corpse now?"

"I took her to her parents' house. They hired me."

And I want to kick myself. I should've seen this coming, but I tend to forget rags have families. "Congratulations. You just saved your life."

"Thank you, sire."

I shoot him in the foot. "Don't steal from me again."

He groans. "Yes, sire."

"Give me the address, then get yourself cleaned up."

"Yes, sire."

From there, I drive back into the city, to a little shack in the Smokestacks. Of course, I put on my respirator before leaving the car.

"Who are you?" the man at the door says.

"Frank Edge," I say. "Adeline was my rag."

"Who's Adeline?"

"Maria."

"Oh. I see. Come in." He sounds like he's about to cry, but he doesn't.

I enter the transition room.

"We'll have to wait here a minute," he says, over the sound of rushing air.

"You fucked with the wrong guy," I say.

"You'll have to speak up."

After a long silence, the man opens the second door, and I enter a small world of vulgarities. I shudder.

These people exist at the bottom of the social Pyramid for a reason.

They don't see themselves as separate from animals, so they cut holes in their floor for plants to grow out of. And their material objects aren't unified by a common theme or idea.

This space speaks only of chaos and neglect.

I feel like tearing this place apart with my bare hands, but for now, I lean against the wall and cross my arms.

"You can take off your mask," the man says, removing his own. "This place is sealed tight."

I don't move.

At this point, the wife approaches me, holding a baby. "Who are you?"

"Frank Edge," I say. "Adeline was my rag."

"Who's Adeline?"

"Maria," the man says.

"I know you have her," I say. "Where is she?"

"She belongs here," the wife says. "You have no right to keep her body."

"I have every right." This is when I take out my knife. "You stole from me, and now I can punish anyone in your household." I point my blade at the baby. "Maybe I'll decide she's the one who masterminded the operation."

"You can't do that."

"Of course I can. I just need to decide if I should take a finger or toe."

The wife yelps, in a strange, unattractive way.

"I told you," the man says, grabbing his wife's arm. "I told you to leave her body alone, but you wouldn't listen. I knew this would happen."

"Don't blame her," I say. "You're the man of this household, and you should've stopped her from disobeying you."

"Please don't hurt our baby," the wife says. "We'll do anything."

"I know." And I put the knife away. "But lucky for you, I'm in a benevolent mood. So I'll leave you unharmed, and I'll give you her body."

"Thank you, sire," says the man.

"Thank you, sire," says the wife.

And I say, "I'd like some time alone with your daughter before I go. Where is she?"

"Behind the bed," the man says, pointing. As if I don't know what a bed is.

"What are you waiting for?" I say. "Go wait outside."

They stare at me for a while, then put on their respirators.

"Don't touch her," the wife says. "Please."

"Don't tell me what to do," I say.

After they're gone, I pull the white sheet off Adeline's body, and I almost don't recognize her. Not because she's dead. Because her hair's braided, and she's wearing jeans and a T-shirt.

She looks so ordinary.

"I'm sorry," I say, and I'm not sure why. Maybe I'm sorry she's dead. Or maybe I'm apologizing for never appreciating her enough when she was alive.

Out of all the Adelines who serviced me in my lifetime, she was the best. I should've told her that when I had the chance.

But it's too late now, and like my father always said, men who dwell on the past are doomed to be conquered by those who see only the future.

I search the room.

In a plastic bag, I find the black dress I bought Adeline for my thirty-fifth birthday. And I find her purse. Inside, there's a pack of cigarettes, a tube of crimson lipstick, and a copy of the script I wrote for last night. I also find a piece of neon paper exhibiting what looks like a phone number.

"Goodbye, Adeline," I say, touching her face. And while I'm used to handling corpses, I shiver, as if the coldness of her body's spreading into mine.

And I see myself lying on the floor, in Adeline's place.

I force myself to laugh.

But somehow, I don't feel any better.

For a few moments, I sit at my desk, smelling the black dress, staring at the empty space where Adeline usually stands.

Fungus of the Heart

Then I dial the number.

One ring later, and a woman says, "Who is this?"

"Frank Edge," I say. "Adeline was my rag."

"Who's Adeline?"

"Maria. Maria Bittencourt. Did you know her?"

"Why?"

"Because I'm trying to find her killer."

The woman doesn't reply.

"Are you still there?" I say.

"Yes," she says.

"Do you know who killed her?"

"That's an interesting question coming from a man like you. Why do you want to know?"

"She was my rag."

"That's not a good enough reason, Mr. Henderson."

So she knows my real name. "She was special to me."

"I find that hard to believe, but for now, I'll give you the benefit of the doubt. We'll continue this conversation in person, tonight at seven. I'll send you the coordinates."

"I'm not meeting with you unless I choose the time and place."

"Then you're not meeting with me."

The phone clicks.

And a few minutes later, I receive the coordinates.

Normally I wouldn't entertain the idea of complying with a woman. Especially a woman as insolent as the one on the phone. But right now, I'm feeling anything but normal.

So at seven o'clock, I'm standing in the middle of the forest, right outside the city, and I remember the hunting trips with my father. Every trip, he taught me new curse words, and we insulted the beasts together.

"Hello, Frank," a woman says, behind me.

I clench my fist, because no woman's ever called me by my first name.

Three women approach. They're all wearing turtlenecks and pants.

"You're late," I say.

The one in the middle hands her lantern to the prettiest girl, and says, "You're lucky we came at all."

"Do you know who killed Adeline?"

"Don't call her that."

"She was my rag, and it was my right to change her name."

"Your laws are only illusions used to maintain your privilege."

"You're a Nymph, aren't you?"

"Why do you say that?"

"Because you sound like one of them. And you wanted to meet in this forest. And your phone number was written on a neon piece of paper."

"I see your point, but I'm not a Nymph. And for your information, I don't sound like one of them. They believe thinking and speaking about laws and politics obstructs the flow of transcendental knowledge."

"What are you then?"

"My name's Fen."

"I didn't ask for your name."

"I'm not here to answer your questions, Frank."

And I can't take this anymore, so I pull out my mag.

But before I can even take aim, Fen grabs my weapon, and points the barrel at my crotch.

I back away. "Wait. Wait a minute."

The pretty girl laughs.

"This isn't funny," Fen says.

"Sorry," the other girl says.

And probably due to the shock of the situation, my defenses weaken, and I almost cry.

This isn't the first time I've had a gun aimed at me, of course. But never by a woman.

"Lie detector," Fen says.

Fungus of the Heart

The uglier girl takes out a small metal box and shines a red light in my eyes.

Fen points my mag at my crotch. "Tell me the truth, and I'll be merciful. Are you really looking for Maria's killer?"

"Yes," I say.

The pretty girl puts a rod in her mouth, which might be a cigarette holder.

Then a dart pierces my chest.

Collapsing, I say, "You fucked with the wrong…"

And when I regain consciousness, everything's spinning. There's blood and women everywhere. They're screaming at me.

Soon, my mind clears, and I realize I'm handcuffed to a hook in the floor. I'm in a windowless room with canisters surrounding me on the floor, and photographs and monitors covering the walls. On one screen, I see a man slicing off a rag's earlobe, over and over. I hear a rag crying, telling a man in a ski mask that the rope is too tight. I see cuts and bruises and bones bursting out of flesh. I see a severed head rolling down the stairs, and I hear a child laughing.

"You look somewhat shocked, Frank," Fen says, sitting on the other side of the room.

"Of course I am," I say. "I didn't know so many men tortured their rags."

"Coming from the man who tortured Maria Bittencourt."

"I never tortured Maria."

"You don't consider rape a form of torture?"

"I never raped her."

"You forced her to have sex with you, under the threat of death."

"I cared for her. And I think she cared for me too."

Fen opens up a briefcase on her lap.

"Could you turn off the monitors?" I say.

"Yes," Fen says. "But I won't."

"I can't hear myself think."

She walks over, carrying a piece of paper, and looks down on me. "This is the waiting list for our detonator-removal operation. About ten percent of women don't survive the procedure, but most of the people I meet add their names to the list. Because they'd take any chance to obtain their freedom from men like you. Here's Maria's signature. She signed four years ago, and if she were still alive, she'd be about two months away from liberation. Her greatest desire was to never see you again, Frank. You made her life a living hell."

I feel dizzy, and I hear a rag begging for mercy. "Turn off the monitors. Please."

"No."

So I close my eyes, but the violence won't disappear. I remember the one time I slapped Adeline. I don't remember why.

"Do you know who killed Adeline?" I say.

"I told you not to call her that," Fen says.

"Do you know who killed Maria?"

"No. Do you have any leads?"

"No."

At this point, the sounds of cruelty stop.

I open my eyes, and I find the monitors muted, and a gun in my face.

"I want to believe in you, Frank," Fen says. "But it's easy for me to look at you and see the men in my past. They were all excellent liars, and I'm sure you are too. There's a good chance you discovered Maria's involvement with my organization, so you killed her, and pretended to search for her killer in order to spark my interest in you. You knew I'd bring you here. Who are you working for? Or is this some vigilante campaign?"

"I wasn't lying to you," I say.

"I wish I could believe that, but I can't take the chance. I'm going to have to kill you, Frank."

"Wait! What about the lie detector? It must've shown you the truth."

"That wasn't a lie detector. That was a box with a red light." She cocks the pistol.

"No!" And like a sissy, my game face crumbles, and I cry.

Fen stares at me in the eyes for a long while. Then she holsters her weapon.

"Thank you," I say, without thinking. I bite my lip, hard.

"You're an egomaniacal psychopath, Frank," Fen says. "But maybe, somehow, there's still some hope for you." She returns to her chair. "I understand your desire to avenge Maria's death, but that's not going to honor her memory, or satisfy her spirit. When I first met Maria, she was a very angry person. She hated you with a passion. But over the years, she worked hard to rise above her feelings of blame to achieve inner peace. What I'm getting at, Frank, is that Maria wouldn't want you to kill for her. She'd want you to help other women like her to attain the freedom she couldn't."

"And how exactly do I do that?"

"There's an underground research facility in the Smokestacks, and they test on women." Fen shows me a photograph of a rag bound to a table, with burn marks all over her naked body. "With the necessary funds, my organization would be more than capable of infiltrating this facility, and liberating the captives."

This is when my tears stop, and my body aches with fury. If I had my gun, someone would be dead by now. "Game's over, sweetheart. You can't swindle a CEO."

"What are you talking about, Frank?"

"You kidnap men and bring them into this torture chamber in order to exploit them out of their hard-earned cash."

"This isn't a torture chamber. This is a cemetery and a space for healing. This room's saved many lives over the years, including my own."

I snicker at the idea.

Then Fen says, "Many of the women who join my organization are suicidal, and require years of emotional and spiritual therapy. One of the most important steps in the road to recovery is to get in touch with your anger. You can't focus on this rage forever, of course, but you can't suppress your feelings either. I created this space because the women in my organization often blame themselves for their experiences. But when they come in here, and see the urns of the dead, and witness the abuses inflicted on others, they're more likely to connect with their inner fury. And for most, this helps them survive."

I snicker again. "You act like you're helping these girls, but you're only manipulating them, so they'll join your little army."

"This isn't an army."

"My point is, these rags don't have any inner fury until you coerce them. You made Maria hate me by showing her these extreme cases."

"They may be extreme, but they're not anomalies. This violence is a direct result of the Pyramid. And if you take part in that system, then you're responsible for even the most extreme consequences." She walks over, and hands me a photograph of Maria. "You didn't kill her, Frank, but you helped maintain the environment that shaped her killer."

I gaze at Maria's smiling face, and my memories of her rally together. "Even if I helped you, and you liberated the rags from that research facility, they'd just get more. Even if you blew up all the facilities in the world, they'd just make more."

"True, but this is part of a greater plan, Frank. Someday we're going to dismantle the Pyramid."

"That's impossible."

"Not if enough people like you help us."

I place the photograph of Maria on the floor, face down. "You're deluding yourself, Fen. You can't change the entire world."

"You only say that because you don't know what we're capable of."

"I do believe you're a special woman, and you're destined to do great things. But you're wasting your time toiling with a bunch of rags. Why don't you come work for me? I can give you real power, and we can show the world what women are really capable of."

"You seem to be under a false impression about me." She removes another paper from her briefcase. "This is the waiting list for our tattoo-removal operation. After my liberation, I had to wait two years before I was unbranded."

"You're a rag?"

"No. But that's what they called me."

And I stare at her forehead, where the symbol used to be, and I feel dizzy again.

Then Fen puts a rod in her mouth.

And collapsing, I say, "I'm sorry."

Maybe the drawers and file cabinets in this office are empty, and maybe I only play a detective in my fantasies. But as I sit here at my fake desk, staring at Maria's photograph, I feel like Frank Edge. A man who always succumbs to a woman's charms, no matter what his gut is telling him.

And right now, my gut's telling me not to press the button on my handheld and transfer a large portion of my fortunes to Fen's account.

Before I can make my decision, someone knocks on my door.

An image of Fen flashes in my head.

But no, it's only Henry.

"What are you doing here?" I say. "Don't tell me the McCarthy deal fell through."

"No, nothing like that. I actually have a confession to make."

"Alright."

Henry sits on Maria's chair, and smiles. "I'm the one who killed her."

"Who?"

"Your rag. Me and Steven and a couple other guys at work planned the whole thing. We set up a series of clues that would eventually lead you to us, but I guess you're a terrible detective." He laughs.

I grab Henry's arms. "You killed Maria?"

"Lighten up, Frank. It was a practical joke."

My fury intensifies, and I scratch Henry's face.

"What's wrong with you, Frank?" Henry says, holding his nose.

I pick up my handheld.

And I can feel my defenses weakening. And if I don't act now, I might actually flip the Pyramid upside down and give the rags the power that's rightfully mine.

So I take out my gun.

"What are you doing?" Henry says.

I fire, right at his forehead.

And I'm at the top of the Pyramid, so the state won't kill me for this.

Instead, they'll send me to the Sanitarium, and I'll be purified of the feelings and ideological poisons surging inside me.

So maybe I am crazy.

But I'm still a man.

The Haunted House

Years ago, back when I could sleep, leviathans and other sea creatures infested my dreams. They never tried to eat me. But their mere presence in a lake or swimming pool or bathtub was always enough to ravage my psyche.

And so, as Rhianna speaks, I see barracuda swimming in and out of her mouth. They taunt me with knowing winks, because I failed in my last barracuda case. But I keep that to myself.

"Did you buy the cranberry sauce?" I say.

"I did," Rhianna says. "And I bought you the crunchy peanut butter and the barbeque chips."

"Rhianna. Those were only alternatives, in case they were out of cranberry sauce."

"I know. But I wanted to make it up to you for calling you Monoxide all those times."

"I've been called worse. And I already told you, I don't take disbelief personally. You found out your water heater was malfunctioning, so it's only natural to assume carbon monoxide poisoning."

"That doesn't excuse my behavior, Ash."

"It does to me."

Rhianna sighs. "Can't we have one conversation that doesn't end up as an argument?"

I rub my face. "I'm sorry. Thanks for all the food."

"You're welcome."

Fungus of the Heart

"So, are you ready?"

"I don't know. I think so. Do you think I'm ready?"

"Of course."

"Are you just saying that to make me feel better?"

"You're a strong woman, Rhianna. And I have complete confidence in you."

"OK. I think I'm ready. I'm ready." She lies back on the bed.

And for a few minutes, I try to work my way inside her. "Do you want me to stop?"

"I don't know."

"We don't have to do this tonight. We've only known each other for a few weeks. And I understand if you're not ready to trust me yet."

"It's not that, Ash. You're one of the most caring people I ever met, and I want to give myself to you. I guess I'm afraid that once you experience the real me, you'll run away screaming."

"Most of my clients feel that way, but I promise you, that won't happen."

"What if I'm worse than everyone else? What if you can't handle me?"

"I've been doing this for eight years, Rhianna. I'm a professional, and I'd rather die a second death than abandon you."

She takes a deep breath. "OK."

And a few seconds later, I'm alive.

I can almost hear the cranberry sauce, peanut butter, and barbeque chips calling out to me, but the first thing I do in Rhianna is strip off all my clothes in front of the full length mirror. Then I spend who knows how long caressing my curves, tracing my stretch marks, tapping my moles.

Rhianna doesn't think of herself as beautiful, but I know better.

I'm perfect.

Downstairs, I eat the cranberry sauce right out of the can, and while Rhianna's palate doesn't appreciate the flavor the way mine used to, I still savor every bittersweet moment.

Before I can even open the peanut butter jar, the otherworld catches up to me. And I'm in two places at once, seeing with two pairs of eyes. I know this because a stuffed octopus hops onto the table.

"Rhianna," the octopus says. "Watch this. Are you watching?"

"I'm watching," I say.

Then the octopus leaps off the table, and twirls all the way to the floor.

"Did you see?" the octopus says.

"I saw," I say. "That was excellent."

"Do you want to try?"

"Maybe later. Right now I'm a little busy."

"OK."

When I open the fridge door to put away the cranberry sauce, a girl in a bloody white dress jumps out at me, waving a knife in my face. I stumble backwards into the table. And a cup falls onto the floor, and shatters.

Glass erupts everywhere.

I've seen girls in bloody white dresses before, of course, though this one's somewhat unique. She's wearing a mask over her face. A little girl mask. And so, I can't be sure she's really a little girl at all.

"Who are you?" I say.

The masked figure growls, tossing the knife from hand to hand.

"Whose blood is that?" I say.

The girl laughs, and runs into the living room, leaving a trail of bloody footprints behind.

I don't know which shards of glass are real, and which aren't. So I avoid them all.

In the living room, I find an enormous chunk of ice hovering above a leather recliner. And if I know one thing about ethereal ice, it's that there's almost always something frozen inside. I can't see what, because the ice is too cloudy, but when I sniff the surface, I detect a faint scent of cinnamon.

"Do you want to play now?" the octopus says, sitting on the leather recliner.

"Not yet," I say.

"Please?"

"Later."

"Please?"

"Alright. We'll play hide and seek. You hide."

"Close your eyes and count to ten."

"Alright."

"Don't peek, OK?"

"I won't."

The octopus scrambles for the kitchen.

And I head upstairs, because I can't melt this hunk of ice on my own.

In the second floor hallway, the masked girl falls from the ceiling and throws a glass knife at me. My instincts kick in, causing me to dodge the weapon, without need. The glass breaks. And once again, the pieces erupt and cover the floor.

This time I know the glass isn't real, because I didn't touch anything, so I step on the shards.

"Who are you?" I say.

The girl runs into the guest bedroom, and I follow.

Inside, the girl's approaching the Man in the Crate.

"Stay away from him," I say. "He's dangerous."

But the girl doesn't listen. She pokes at one of the holes in the crate, and he snatches the knife away from her.

The girl growls.

"Give that back to her," I say.

"If you say so," the Man says.

Then the knife flies out of the hole, and slices the girl's shoulder. She barks at the man before sprinting out of the room.

"You have to stop impeding my investigations," I say.

"I'll stop when you let me out," the Man says.

"That's never going to happen."

"Then I'm never going away."

"You don't belong here."

"Of course not. I belong at home with my wife and son, but you locked me up in a fucking crate."

Years ago, back when I lived with my parents, my father frequently received crates for his business. He opened them inside the house, and he held me up, so I could get the first look at the contents.

"What do you see?" my father said.

And I described the artwork as best I could.

But one day, I didn't say a word. Because all my attention was on the dead possum at the bottom of the crate. I imagined myself trapped in the small space, starving, dying of thirst.

At the time, I cried, horrified by the thought. But now, I wish the Man could suffer the possum's fate.

"You have two options," the man says. "One. You can let me out now, and I'll go easy on you. Or two. You can keep being a coward, and someday soon I'll bust out of here. And I'll rip your fucking head off."

"You need to accept the fact that there's no escape for you."

"Yeah? Take a look at this." He thrusts his muscular arm through one of the holes, and flexes his bicep. "I've been pumping iron in here nonstop."

"That won't help you."

"We'll see, won't we?"

I try to laugh away the thought, but I'm still terrified he's right. "You've wasted enough of my time. I'm leaving."

"I'm not done with you yet."

"I don't care." And I step over a crowbar.

"Come back here, you crazy bitch!"

I close the door behind me.

There's no activity in the hallway, so I enter the master bedroom, where I discover a middle-aged woman strapped to what looks like a hospital bed. She struggles. And the masked girl tosses a glass vase at my feet.

"Please don't do this," the woman says.

The girl picks up a shard of glass, which transforms into a knife.

"Help me!" the woman says, looking at me.

"I can't," I say. "I'm sorry."

The girl hops onto the table, and sits on the woman's stomach. Then she begins cutting the woman's wrists.

"Stop!" the woman says, flooding the room with blood.

The girl laughs.

"Who are you?" I say.

"You know who I am," the woman says.

I wade through the blood and lean in close. "If you answer my questions, I'll help you get away from her."

"OK."

"Who are you?"

"I'm your sister. Meghan."

"Why are you in a hospital bed?"

"I tried to kill myself two years ago."

"Who is this girl?"

"I don't know, but she looks like you when you were a child."

The blood level rises above my eyes, and everything's red, and I smell cinnamon.

I turn to the girl. "I think it's time we take off that mask."

The girl swims away.

And I follow. Downstairs, the girl's sitting on the leather recliner, switching her knife from hand to hand.

"You shouldn't play with her," the octopus says, on top of the TV. "She's not nice. Why don't we watch the princess movie instead?" He presses a tape into the VCR, and on the screen, there's Rhianna in a white dress, riding on a unicorn.

I kneel in front of the recliner. "I'd like to see your face."

The girl snarls, and points her weapon at me.

But I don't move. "You need to show me."

"No."

"Please."

"No!" The girl turns away from me. "I'm a monster."

"Why do you say that?"

"You saw what I did to Meghan."

"That wasn't real, Rhianna. You'd never hurt your sister like that."

"You don't know what I'm capable of."

"Actually, I do. I also know you're uncomfortable in that mask. There aren't any holes to see or breathe through. Why don't you take it off for just a little while?"

"If I do, you'll want to kill me."

"I won't. I promise."

"You're a liar." She doesn't sound too sure of herself.

Therefore, I take this opportunity to reach out.

She stabs my hand, over and over, but I don't stop.

I can't really touch her, of course, though part of her wants me to see her. And so, I'm able to pull off the mask.

"Don't look at me!" the girl says, covering her face with her hands.

I pick up the hand mirror that appears on the coffee table. "Look, Rhianna."

"No!"

"You're not a monster, Rhianna. Look."

She does. And she sees that underneath the mask of the little girl, there's a little girl.

"I don't understand," Rhianna says.

"You will," I say.

Without the mask obstructing her eyes, Rhianna cries, and the ice above her begins to melt.

"I think you should move," I say.

Rhianna takes my advice just in time.

Because the chunk of ice splits in half, and an old man falls onto the recliner. The two pieces of ice shatter on the floor, while the man stands, carrying a snowball.

He heads upstairs.

I glance at the spot where Rhianna was standing, but she's already gone.

So I follow the man.

And with every step, my terror intensifies, ravaging my psyche. In my last barracuda case, this is the point when I failed. I let the fear get the better of me, and my client forced me out of her prematurely, and she refused to let me back in.

I hug my chest. "Everything's gonna be alright."

When I reach the upstairs hallway, I sit on the floor and breathe, deep.

"Let's play in the backyard," the octopus says, beside me. "You can be the mommy, and I'll be the baby."

"I can't play right now," I say.

"OK."

"Did you see which room the old man went into?"

"You shouldn't play with him. He's not nice. How about you be the baby, and I'll be the mommy?"

I notice the frost on the doorknob of Rhianna's childhood bedroom. I stand.

"You can't go in there," the octopus says.

"I have to," I say.

Then the octopus opens his maw, and reveals barracuda-like teeth. He vomits out a cluster of slimy cobras and tarantulas. And while I'm not particularly frightened of these creatures, Rhianna's a different story.

Out of instinct, I close my eyes, but of course this doesn't help. Rhianna can still see with my perception, and nothing can block my vision.

I feel faint. "Don't do this."

The octopus upchucks another batch. "Play with me in the backyard and I'll get rid of them."

The bonds holding me and my body together are deteriorating fast, so I hurry toward the bedroom. But the door's now coated with snakes and spiders.

I'm afraid touching the doorknob would push Rhianna over the edge.

So I face the octopus. "I know what you're trying to do, and I appreciate your concern for your friend. But I'm not her. I'm a spiritual being named Ash."

"You mean like a ghost?" the octopus says.

"Yeah."

"But ghosts are just pretend, remember? Your mom said they're hallucinations caused by carbon monoxide poisoning."

"Well, she was wrong."

"You don't look like a ghost."

"That's because...." And I stop myself, because there's no point arguing with a defense mechanism. This octopus only has one thing on his mind, and that's what I need to exploit. "If you don't dispose of these creatures, I'm going to throw this body down the stairs and break my neck."

The octopus rubs the top of his head. "I don't understand this game, Rhianna."

"This isn't a game."

And after the snakes and spiders turn to glass, I turn the doorknob and reach my destination.

In the bedroom, the old man paces back and forth between two beds. And on each bed is a little girl.

The old man's smiling, tossing a snowball from hand to hand.

After a while, Rhianna hops off the bed.

And the old man throws the snowball at her face. "I told you not to move!"

Rhianna cries.

I want to hold her, comfort her. But I can't.

The old man picks up Rhianna and drops her on the bed. Then he takes a glass unicorn off the dresser. He acts he's going to throw this at Rhianna as well, but he smashes the figurine on the wood floor instead. He laughs.

"Are you ready for some fun, Meghan?" the old man says.

Meghan doesn't move or say a word, and the old man climbs onto her bed, and the dog in the room growls.

Rhianna hugs her octopus, tight.

I've seen enough.

And so, I leave Rhianna's body, and she collapses to the floor, weeping and heaving.

I put my hand on her shoulder, though I know she can't feel me. "I'm sorry."

A few minutes later, she looks me in the eyes. "I should've helped her."

"You were a child."

"I should've saved her."

"It's not your fault."

She curls up, tight.

And maybe she feels broken, but I know better.

Now that she remembers the truth, she can stop blaming herself for what happened to her sister.

She can heal.

Hours later, Rhianna sits up. "Everything we saw tonight makes a strange sort of sense to me, except for that guy in the box. Why did his voice sound like you?"

"He has nothing to do with you," I say. "I'm sorry he showed up like that."

"Who is he?"

"I don't discuss him with clients."

"But he showed up during my investigation. Don't I have a right to know?"

"No."

Rhianna sighs. "Are we going to spend the rest of our time together fighting?"

I run my hands down my face. "Alright. I'll tell you."

"Thank you."

I stare at the crowbar beside my foot. "First you need to know that years ago, back when I was alive, I realized I was a woman in a man's body."

"Oh."

"But I never told anybody. And I didn't even let myself think about it very much. All my life, I acted like the man everyone expected me to be. And when I died, the façade I created became the Man in the Crate. I don't let him dictate my behavior anymore, but I can't seem to get rid of him either."

"I'm sorry."

"Thanks. It's not so bad though. I'm happy enough with my existence."

"If that's true, then why do you sound so sad?"

"Well, I guess I'm not completely content. I know my appearance is only an ethereal shadow of physical reality, but I hate looking like this."

"Like a man?"

"Yeah."

"There's no way to change how you look after you die?"

"Well, some spirits change. But I don't think I can."

"Why not?"

"Because I'm not strong enough."

And as hopelessness wreaks havoc on my soul, the Man in the Crate manifests beside me.

He slams his body against the wood. "Let me out, you fucking wacko!"

I know he's keeping me from changing my form. And I know I should confront him once and for all. But I'm afraid if I open the crate, he'll overpower me, and crush everything inside me I hold dear.

"Ash," Rhianna says. "Just because you feel powerless doesn't mean you are."

Maybe she's right.

And maybe one day I'll face my fears.

But for now, I decide to ignore the Man in the Crate, and watch Rhianna cry.

Fungus of the Heart

The smart thing would be to ignore the jester as he taunts me with a slap of his ass and a lick of the bloody saw attached to his marotte. But I stopped making wise decisions ever since they locked you up in the Fortress. Anyway, the clown butchered Billy, and you know how much I love that warthog.

So I run after the maniac.

And he leads me through a forest that reminds me of your fuzzy green boots, because of all the moss.

If I exerted myself, I could catch up to the fleet-footed fool in a matter of moments. But of course I'm not willing to sacrifice even a smidgen of my true power. Not for anyone but you.

Eventually, the harlequin leaps on a heap of trash, and rolls around, giggling.

"Why did you murder my companion?" I say.

The jester ignores me.

So I race over, and kick him in the stomach. "I said, why did you murder my companion?"

"I heard you." He speaks, barely moving his lips, using his marotte like a ventriloquist dummy. The scepter's topped with a small, wooden version of the jester's head, with matching donkey ears, scars. Even the same frown line.

He still doesn't answer my question, so I kick him again.

"You looked so peaceful," the fool says. "Lying there on the grass, all cuddly-wuddly with the piggy. I knew you loved him."

"So you drugged me in my sleep?" I say. "And you sawed off his head?"

"I had to do something. The bond between you and the beast reeked in my mind's nostril. Just thinking about it makes me throw up in my mouth. Blerg! Blerg!"

"Stop that."

"No. Blerg!"

I stomp on his hand. "The more you annoy me, the less merciful I feel. I suggest you beg Billy for forgiveness, or I'll have no problem ridding the world of a speciesist like you."

The jester raises an eyebrow. "Speciesist? You misunderstand my sentiment. I don't have a particular prejudice against the camaraderie between man and beast. I abhor all emotional connections, equally."

"Ah. So you're one of the Void."

The marotte head nods.

And I grab the real clown's throat. "One of your kind tortured and killed my five-year-old niece."

He grins. "Good."

The grief smoldering in my muscles suddenly blazes, causing me to punch the jester in his face, over and over.

He rolls away, stands. Attacks me with his saw.

But I kick the scepter out of his hands, and continue the onslaught.

Finally, he says, "Stop it! Stop!"

And I comply. "I don't understand you. If you truly believe the so-called material world is meaningless, then why would you want to protect yourself? Isn't your body as meaningless as everything else?"

"Of course! Jeez. But you're inflicting pain for the wrong reasons. Abuse and murder should be about breaking free from the chains of morality. In other words, you should only kill when you feel unjustified and devoid of bloodlust. Anything else is a sin."

"So you're trying to protect me from sinning?"

He nods. "Have mercy on yourself. Please. Let me go."

I know you taught me not to utilize my abilities for the sake of vengeance, but this clown needs dire consequences for his actions.

He needs to die.

Then again, this man is one of the Void, and that means he's already suffered a fate worth than death.

So with a compassionate heart, I break both his legs, and leave it at that.

On my way out of the clearing, the man grunts. Louder and louder.

At first I think he's imitating Billy in an attempt to harass me.

But then I turn around and see Billy soaring over the pile of trash. He touches down in front of me.

"What are you doing here?" I say, smiling. "I thought you'd be halfway to the Heavens by now."

The clown takes a break from his weeping to say, "There are no Heavens. When your piggy ascends, he'll wander around in empty space for the rest of eternity."

I ignore him.

And Billy releases a long blissful grunt as I stroke him behind the ear. The massage doesn't last nearly as long as usual, because he's only a winged head now, and I can't touch his shoulders and back.

"I'm sorry you died," I say. "I failed you."

The warthog doesn't move, showing me there are no hard feelings.

Then he hops over to the trash, and begins rooting.

I wait, cross-legged.

Finally, Billy calls me over with a lengthy grumble, and I pick up the hairbrush by his snout.

He barks at me.

"Sorry," I say, and pick up the other object by his nose.

A broken key.

Billy doesn't bark this time, so this must be what he wants to show me.

And I know better than to search for the lock this key opens, because I worked for a fallen angel six months ago, and I learned more than a little about his kind.

The first lesson being, angels almost always communicate in metaphors. Symbols.

So I say, "Does the fact that the key is broken hold any special significance? Or was this just the only key you could find?"

Billy grunts, then barks. The condition of the key is important.

"Are you referring to something that can't be opened or penetrated?"

Yes.

"Is this concerning an object of some sort?"

No.

"An entryway?"

Yes. Then he presses his snout against my foot. A kiss.

This message is about you.

"Does the key represent my present inability to reach Cailin?"

Yes.

"Don't worry, Billy. I won't start the war before I'm ready. I know I need another mushroom before I stand a chance of saving her."

He repositions his ears, upset. Maybe he doesn't want me to fight at all.

"I appreciate your concern and I realize your new form gives you a greater awareness of the dangers I'm about to face. But this is something I have to do. I'm sure you understand."

But apparently, he doesn't. Because he takes off again, barks. Feints at me with his snout.

"Calm down," I say.

Then Billy lands beside the clown and continues rooting. Probably for another symbolic piece of trash.

"You're a good friend, and I know you mean well. But I can't stay here playing Twenty Questions all day. Cailin needs me."

So I turn around.

And Billy screams, as if he's in pain. But I know that's impossible in his state. He's just trying to garner my sympathies.

"Maybe your piggy's an angel of death," the jester says. "Piss him off too much, and he'll kill your Cailin. Gobble her all up."

I want to silence the clown, comfort my friend.

But I ignore them both, and walk away.

Of course I do.

For you, I'd do anything.

Like always, I quickly assess the village's prosperity by discerning the quality of laughter in the air. And these villagers definitely scream of wealth, with their carefree cackles and hearty chuckles.

They don't have raiders on the communal mind.

And that means there's a Protector here. Somewhere.

So I blow some truth pollen at a toothless old man, and join him on the stump.

"You're quite handsome," he says. "I'd like to kiss you, but I'm afraid you wouldn't let me."

"I'm sorry," I say. "My lips belong to another."

He frowns. "You're only saying that to spare my feelings. You think I'm ugly."

"That's not true. My Cailin is an elder, like you, and she's the most beautiful thing in all the worlds."

The old man grins. "I can't remember the last time I spoke to a romantic. Four years? Five? It's good to know your breed isn't extinct."

His eyes appear fully dilated at this point, so I say, "Do you have a Protector in your village?"

"Yes. It's funny. Milena was such a troublemaker in her youth. One summer, about twenty years ago, our soulstones started disappearing. Everyone was sure someone had awoken a demon. But then Fortunata, Milena's mother, found the stones in a dead toad in Milena's hut. Everyone despised the girl. Myself included. At that time, we didn't know about her power, and so we didn't understand her confusion and her suffering. We barely spoke to her. Even her parents avoided her. Then, years later, she revealed her true nature to us, and now she's our beloved Protector. I'm still surprised she's willing to sacrifice so much for those who treated her with such cruelty. But I suppose she has a heart for forgiveness. I can't say the same for myself."

"Where does Milena live?"

He points. "On the outskirts."

"Thank you."

Tears roll down the old man's face, dirty with pollen. "Poor little girl. I know I wasn't her relative, but I could've reached out to her. I could've shown her some kindness. Maybe I should apologize to her now."

"Yes. You should."

With that, I squeeze the old man's shoulder, gently, and head for the outskirts.

And as the woodland becomes denser, so does my mind.

Memories stalk my conscience. Broken bodies. Shrieks and pleas and the taste of toadstools and blood.

I try not to look these phantoms in the eyes. Instead, I keep my gaze focused on their elbows. Their fingernails. And somehow, by limiting my perception, I can almost convince myself they're not human beings. They're just bundles of flesh, no greater than the sum of their parts.

But the illusion won't keep me moving.

Not for long.

I need to hear your voice. I need to know you'll still want me, even after I accomplish my mission.

And then, finally, you say, "I'll always love you."

And my conviction prevails, overshadowing the phantoms once more.

"I love you too."

A heartbeat later, Billy swoops down, grunts. Lands beside a glittery web that stretches between two trees.

The warthog points his snout at the pastel spider and her quivering prey.

"Is this what you think is going to happen to me when I break into the Fortress?"

He barks a no.

"Then I'm represented by the spider?"

No.

"Again, I'm grateful that you care about me, but I don't have time to decipher your doubts and fears about my future."

Billy protests.

And I'm about to start walking again when the monkey reaches out to me with a tiny hand.

Of course, I know I shouldn't save her. I shouldn't upset the natural balance.

But right now, I don't care.

Sometimes I need to do the wrong thing and be the hero.

The fiery flowers dominating the meadow remind me of the robe you wore during my training lessons. And Milena's dwelling, a bulge in center of the clearing, brings to mind our unborn child.

I try not to think about his fate, but of course, the resistance only intensifies my focus on the tragedy.

They took him from you right after he was born. Perhaps before. And if he's still alive, I'm sure he's one of them by now.

A soldier who would sacrifice his life to annihilate people like us.

The door opens and a woman approaches me, and I'm thankful for the distraction from my thoughts.

After a few moments, I'm sure she's Milena. She's not wearing the traditional garb of a Protector, but she walks like one. Swift, calm. Confident in her ability to survive.

She stops about five paces from me. "Who are you?"

"My name's Nightingale," I say.

"Seriously?"

"Yes."

"Who sent you?"

"No one. I'm here to offer you my services as a Sentinel."

She swats at the idea with her hand. "I don't need any help."

"Of course you don't. But this isn't about need, Milena. This is about what you deserve. When was the last time you had a good day's sleep?"

She shrugs. "That's not important."

"You only think that way because you've been taught to sacrifice yourself for your village."

"No. It doesn't count as sacrifice if your beneficiaries repay you for your good deeds."

"But they don't pay you nearly enough. I've worked for enough Protectors to know that."

Milena sighs. "Debate me all you want. I'm not about to put up some outsider just so he can play sandman for me."

"You wouldn't say that if you remembered what it's like to experience deep slumber. But I'd bet my soulstone the last time you slept like a baby was as a baby. So why not give me a chance first, then make your decision as to the value of my assistance. I was trained in the defensive arts by Cailin Airfist, and I promise you, I can keep you safe."

She stares at me, and bites her fingernail. "I can't take your word for that. I'll need references."

"Of course."

"Let's go inside."

And Milena's underground cottage shocks my senses.

Vivid colors, bizarre forms, complex smells.

At first, I can't perceive beyond the entirety of the space.

Then my eyes dart about, out of control, and I see an armless goddess with golden lips, luminescent snake bones dangling from the ceiling, cerulean candles shaped like vulvas, a collection of twig dolls with hornet nest heads.

"Are these all protective charms?" I say.

"Yes." Milena sets her scrying bucket on a low table.

"There has to be at least a hundred types of fetishes in here. But most villages only produce five, ten varieties."

"True."

Despite my curiosity, I drop the subject. I can tell she's not prepared to give me any substantial information about her life. Not yet.

She hands me a needle.

And I prick my finger, bleed into the bucket.

Wait.

Obviously, this cluttered cottage bears no resemblance to our simple hut, but I can't help thinking of home anyway. I can almost see you kneeling on the floor, eyes closed, lips trembling. Sometimes I only pretended to meditate with you, and I watched you instead.

My memories scatter as the water in the bucket rises.

And Milena asks my past employers the usual questions, triggering the usual answers.

Eventually, she finishes with the last Protector, and stares at me. "You have no recent references. Why?"

"I haven't worked for a while," I say.

"Why would I hire you if no one else will? Maybe you've lost your touch."

"The only reason no one hired me is because I spent the last year alone in a cave. Grieving. The Army captured Cailin, took her to the Fortress. She and I are bound by the heart."

"I see. I'm sorry."

"Thank you."

"You're sure you're ready to start working again?"

"Yes. Cailin wouldn't want me to hide from my life forever. She spent years imbuing me with her skills and knowledge, and I don't intend to waste that gift."

Milena laughs. "Why you Sentinels train so hard just so you can help us Protectors sleep, I'll never understand."

"I can help you understand, if you let me."

She rubs her forehead. "Fine."

"First of all, learning the defensive arts isn't merely a means of obtaining a place in the worlds. That's only a physical manifestation of our spiritual metamorphosis. But there's so much more to our art than what can be seen. So much more than I could ever explain with words or thoughts."

"Alright. But why use your skills to protect Protectors? Why don't you become Protectors yourselves?"

"Simple. Unlike your people, my people can be conquered. Yes, we're strong in spirit and body, but your power will always surpass ours and anyone else's in the corporeal realm. As a Protector, you prevent most conflict by your mere presence. But if Sentinels attempted to infiltrate your niche, we'd only end up instigating more violence. Therefore, we accept our place as servants and guardians to the guardians."

"I guess that makes sense. Still, seems like a waste of potential to me. But who am I to talk?"

"You're a Protector."

She shrugs, picks a piece of lint off her plain grey tunic. Stands. "I need to start breakfast. Or dinner, in your case."

I stand too, smiling. "Why don't you let me cook for us? In my home village, I'm actually quite renowned for my abilities as a chef."

"No."

"All my past employers were happy with my cooking. I can resummon them if you don't believe me."

"I believe you. But it's not about talent. I just...like my food my way."

"OK."

"You can put your things in the storage room. Feel free to pile up all my junk in the corners."

"Thank you." I smile.

She doesn't.

Once she's inside the kitchen, I take a deep breath.

Then I enter my new room, and curl up on the floor, waiting for the phantoms to return.

Two weeks in, Protectors usually start to trust me while they sleep. But Milena still springs to vigilance every time I test her with a cough or a sneeze. And while I'm confident her desire for security will eventually spark a bond between us, so far we only seem to be moving further and further apart. In fact, at this point, she barely speaks a word to me during those few hours when we're both awake at the same time.

This morning, she says, "There's a seraphic boar making a fuss outside. He's no angel of mine, but he wouldn't give me a moment's peace. Is he yours?"

My heart assaults my chest. "What did he say?"

"I don't know. I don't speak warthog."

"Would you mind if I borrowed one of your sacred blades?"

She shakes her head, and carries her basket of herbs into the kitchen.

Outside, Billy drops a slimy stone at my feet.

But I ignore the message. "Were you trying to tell Milena the truth about me?"

His eyes expose a struggle in his mind. Maybe he's trying to lie to me, but he can't. Not in his current form. So he grunts an affirmative.

"Do you realize what would happen if she discovered the truth? If she didn't kill me, she'd at least toss me out, and I'd have to start Phase Six over again. Is this really what you want? You'd rather I die or fail than do what must be done?"

Yes.

I sigh. "I love you, Billy, and I don't want to see you go. But I can't let anyone jeopardize my mission. I hope you understand."

Another yes.

And with the sacred blade, I cut the thread between his heart and mine. Of course, when dealing with angels, any symbolic act results in physical consequences.

So the connection anchoring Billy to the physical realm severs. And he screams, spiraling out of control into the Heavens.

"Goodbye."

I'm ashamed to admit this, but I'm not only relieved to see him go. I'm happy.

In life, Billy was an ideal companion. No matter what I did or didn't do, he never looked down on me. Never judged me. But his death changed the nature of our relationship.

I'm better off without him.

I know I should ignore Billy's final message, but my curiosity triumphs over reason in a matter of moments. So I kneel and examine the object at my feet.

And in the stone, I see a dragon, ready to strike.

I don't need to ask any questions to understand the warning. If I succeed in my mission, I'll become a monster.

But, of course, I knew this long ago. The creature I'm destined to become haunts my nightmares, and he's much more of a monster than any dragon.

Stronger. Bigger. More grotesque.

As I rub the dragon with my thumb, the residue of Billy's compassion and loyalty warms my soul. I know he only wants what's best for me.

However, my life isn't about me anymore.

My life is, and always will be, yours.

At first, my sleepy eyes widen with the fear of phantoms. But no, these voices refrain from clawing at my eardrums.

So I follow the sound to the living room, and stare through the crack in Milena's door.

She's sitting on the rug, biting her fingernails, across from a man in a black cape.

"We tried rationing the food evenly," the man says, his voice shaking. "But that yielded only widespread malnutrition, illness, death. So we started a lottery system to decide who lives and who dies. I'm one of the lucky ones, but my son…he doesn't have much time left. I try to give him food, but he won't accept." He wipes his snot and tears with his sleeve. "He's planning a raid on your village. He's already recruited about thirty doomed members from my band."

"Don't worry," Milena says. "I'll send them running back home before any blood can be spilled."

The man shakes his head. "I'm afraid they won't give up so easily. They're planning on blinding themselves before the battle, so as not to be intimidated by you."

Milena sighs. "Sight or no, there's no ignoring my power. They'll still feel me in their bones. Tell them that."

"They're beyond desperate, Milena, and there's no stopping them. Not without bloodshed. But if you give us more food, maybe you can prevent the massacre."

"I'm sorry. I've got nothing to spare."

He gestures at the bags behind her. "What about those?"

"I have four more bands to feed."

"Please, Milena. I'll do anything. My people will do anything."

"I know. I wish I could do more for you, but I can't."

He stabs the air, pointing his finger at the bags again. "Of course you can!"

"Do you want me to create my own lottery system? I could choose one band to feed, at random, and give the others nothing. Are you prepared to lose my patronage completely for a chance to gain more?"

The man rubs his beard for a while, then shakes his head.

"I'm sorry about your son, Arthur," Milena says. "I'll do everything I can to repel him without force."

"It doesn't matter," Arthur says. "He'll soon be dead anyway."

"Maybe not. Maybe he'll find a way."

"You're a fool." And with that, Arthur sets a twig doll by her knee, and walks out of the room, cradling his bag of food like a newborn child.

After the front door slams, Milena cries. So soft, I can barely hear her.

This is my chance.

So I enter the room, without permission, and wrap my arm around her.

"What are you doing?" Milena says.

"My job," I say.

"Your job is to help me sleep."

"And that's exactly what I'm doing. If I don't comfort you, your spirit will keep crying out for support. And that's not exactly the ideal condition for a sound slumber."

"My spirit isn't crying out for anything."

"Of course she is. Your sorrow manifests as tears so that others can perceive your feelings and react accordingly. Now stop arguing, and let me do my job."

And for a few minutes, Milena allows me to hold her.

Then she walks into the living room, places the twig doll with the others. Sits.

I join her at the table. "You're the first Protector I've known who gives food to raiders."

"Calling them raiders dehumanizes them," Milena says. "They're just people. Unlucky people."

"You're right. I'm sorry."

She sips her cold tea. "I lied to Arthur. I told him there was nothing more I could do for him. But I could coerce more food from my villagers. Terrorize them into submission."

"Why don't you?"

"Because I'm selfish and pathetic and I want my villagers to like me."

"You want a home. There's nothing wrong with that."

"Of course there is. My desire for belonging kills people."

"You're not responsible for everyone around you, Milena."

"Then why do I have so much power?"

"Because you were born that way."

She takes another drink. "You're making excuses for my behavior because you want me to feel better. You don't really believe what you're saying."

"Actually, I do. In this life, sometimes you have to choose your own wellbeing over someone else's. Because if you surrender too much of yourself, you'll lose your altruistic spirit altogether, and then you won't be of any use to anyone."

"I don't believe any of that."

"You don't want to believe it, but you know I'm right."

"Please stop trying to defend me, Nightingale."

"Someone has to. As it is, you're on a path of self-destruction. And if you don't free yourself from your guilt soon, you'll be eaten alive from the inside."

"Maybe that's what I deserve."

"What you deserve is happiness and health. You deserve a good day's sleep. A hearty meal. Let me cook for you."

She shakes her head. "I like my cooking."

"You like starving yourself with portions unfit for a squirrel, because you can't stand the thought of nourishing yourself while there are those who can't."

Milena stands. "I hate to cut the pep talk short, but I need to start dinner."

"At least let me help."

"No."

"Tomorrow?"

"You don't give up, do you?"

"No."

And as she laughs, I'm that much closer to breaking her.

Milena sleeps with one eye open. But still, I'm making progress.

With each passing day, she talks more, eats more. Even smiles more.

Today, she says, "When I was sixteen, I revealed my nature to my parents. I told them I needed to find another Protector to teach me about my power. So I left, and found a Protector willing to help me. After a few weeks of training, he tried to rape me. I'm sure he thought he could overpower me, since I still didn't know how to control my abilities very well. But I killed him. I didn't mean to. I don't think I meant to. Anyway, I had no intention of returning here. I hated my parents, and everyone in my community. So after I killed Daniel, I wandered around from village to village, searching for a new home. But none of them would grant me citizenship."

"I don't see how that's possible," I say. "Everyone wants a Protector."

"I wanted to find a group who liked me for who I am, not what I am. So I told them I wouldn't use my power under any circumstances. They begged and pleaded for me to change my mind, of course, but I wouldn't waver in my determination. Eventually, they grew bitter, and banished me. This happened over and over. No one wanted me, so I returned here."

"I'm sorry."

"Yeah, well. At least my naiveté didn't get me killed. I'm lucky."

"You shouldn't minimalize the pain of your past."

"You'd rather I wallow in self-pity?"

"I'm merely suggesting that you practice self-empathy. Because if you're not a friend to yourself, then you're an enemy. And that's no way to live."

Then, out of nowhere I can imagine, Milena kisses me.

But don't worry. The tentacles of warmth extending from my stomach don't mean a thing. Her lips simply remind me of yours.

"I belong to Cailin," I say.

"I know," Milena says. "I'm sorry."

"If that's true, then why are you smiling?"

"Sometimes I smile when I'm embarrassed."

"Just don't let it happen again."

Milena nods, and escapes into the kitchen with the dishes.

Soon, I'm asleep in my bedroom as my dreamself vomits blood into a scrying bucket on the table.

The water boils, rises. Transforms into the Imposter.

I try to walk away, but my feet root into the floor. "You don't give up, do you?"

"No," she says. "I need to talk to you."

"I've never fallen for your trickery before. What makes you think you'll succeed this time?"

"Just hear me out. Please?"

"I don't actually have choice in the matter, do I?"

"I suppose not."

"Then let's get this over with."

The Imposter plays with a long ashen braid. "I just...I want you to know I won't mind if you give yourself to Milena. I know how you feel about her."

Fungus of the Heart

"You don't know anything. I belong only to Cailin, and I wish you'd stop trying to interfere with our relationship."

"For the last time, Night. I am Cailin."

I shake my head. "You're nothing but a shadow who preys on people's hearts."

The Imposter sighs. "If you won't let yourself love Milena, at least promise me you won't go through with your mission."

"I'll promise you nothing, nightfiend."

And before the soulsucker can respond, a hand reaches out from the scrying bucket. My hand. Only stronger. Bigger. More grotesque.

The monster I'm destined to become pulls the Imposter down into the blood.

She reaches out to me with your familiar hand.

And I feel like saving her. Everything about her reminds me of you.

But I let the monster consume her.

Of course I do.

For you, I'd devour anyone.

※

Just as Milena climbs into bed, a young girl peeks into the bedroom. For all I know, she's one of those child warriors from the west, so I enter a battle stance.

"Come in, Hada," Milena says, smiling.

And I return to a relaxed position.

"I made you this," Hada says, and hands over a soap carving of a dog, perhaps.

"Thank you so much," Milena says.

"She's an elephant."

"I'll cherish her always."

"What about when you burn her all up?"

"I'll still cherish her."

"Do you know my cousin Abran?"

"Yeah."

"Abran says that lion candles are better than elephant candles, but I don't think so."

"I don't think so either."

Hada grins. "I gotta go now, because I told my mom I'd help her with the corn."

"Alright."

She bows. "Thank you for your protection."

"Thank you for your cuteness."

Hada giggles and rushes away.

"I know she's only a child," I say. "But even she should know better than to enter someone's dwelling without knocking."

"Don't patronize her, please." Milena sets the elephant on her nightstand. "Hada's an intelligent girl, and she was following my orders. I've told all the children in the village they can enter my home at any time. No permission necessary."

"And you didn't think to inform me of this?"

"I didn't think you'd mistake a child for a threat."

"Now who's patronizing children? They can be just as dangerous as adults, under certain circumstances."

Milena sighs. "Fine. I should've told you. Happy?"

"I'll be happy when you start sleeping soundly through the day."

"You're one to talk, with all the nightmares. You talk in your sleep. Scream, sometimes."

"I'm sorry."

"Don't apologize."

"I'll sleep outside from now on."

"That's ridiculous, Nightingale."

"It's my job to relieve you of stress. And listening to someone yelling isn't exactly relaxing."

"I like knowing someone's in the house with me. It's...comforting."

"OK. But the offer's still open, if you change your mind."

"I won't." Milena lies back in her bed, and usually she turns away from me at once. But this time, she watches me as I stand vigil at her beside. "I've never seen a Sentinel in action. Would you show me some moves?"

"OK."

So I perform for her, invoking the spirits of stone and wood, fighting invisible enemies throughout the room.

Afterward, Milena claps. "It's almost like dancing."

"Almost," I say.

Then she rolls away.

Hours later, a nude man in a necktie crawls into the cottage. A smirk on his face and a briefcase balanced on his back.

I still haven't tested Milena tonight, so I remain hidden behind the door.

The nude man lies on his stomach beside the bed. Grabs the suitcase. Stands.

And as he raises the suitcase above his head, Milena's eyes open.

Of course, that's my cue to tackle him.

"Why did you let him get so close?" she says.

I begin hogtying the man. "I didn't want to immobilize him until I knew his intent."

"You could've stopped him first and asked questions later."

"People lie. Actions don't."

"Everything lies," the man says.

"This suitcase is filled with rocks," Milena says, lifting the weapon. "He could've killed me."

"Life is death," the man says.

I touch Milena's arm. "You weren't in any danger. I'd never let anyone hurt you."

She kneels beside the man. "I know what you've heard about Protectors, but I'm willing to give your band food in exchange for an armistice. If I let you go, will you relay my offer?"

The man giggles.

"What's so funny?" Milena says.

"You offer us food," he says. "But my people never go hungry with so many sinners around."

"He's not a raider," I say. "He's of the Void."

"I'm not familiar with that clan," Milena says.

"If there's more of them around, they'll torture and kill your villagers without hesitation."

"And we'll gobble them all up," the man says. "Though sometimes we have to throw up some people so we can keep eating the rest. But I think that still counts, right?"

Milena sprints all the way to the village core, and I barely keep up.

"These Void," Milena says. "How many are there?"

"I don't know," I say. "It's more of a movement than an actual group. They often travel alone, but sometimes—"

And the horde of Void skipping out of the forest finishes my sentence for me. They're all nude. Neckties. Briefcases.

The nearby villagers stand and stare. Some of them laugh.

I enter a battle stance, but I don't attack.

Because Milena's already projecting her power.

Thousands of teal threads of energy erupt from her body and squirm in the air. After Milena screams, the strands burst into flame. Then the glowing strings whip forward and point at the horde.

But the Void keep coming.

"Why aren't they scared?" Milena says.

"I'm sure they are," I say. "They just don't care."

"What do I do?"

"What do you mean?"

Fungus of the Heart

"I don't want to touch them."

"OK. I'll handle them."

"You can't fight all of them. Can you?"

"I don't know."

But I try. I inhale the spirits in the air, and let them guide me. Out of the corner of my eye, I can see you fighting alongside me. Protecting me. But no, you're in the Fortress, because when you really needed me, I couldn't protect you.

And I can't protect this village either.

There's too many Void, and I can't incapacitate them fast enough.

"No!" Milena says.

I turn my head in time to see one of her threads brush a nude man's face. He shrieks. Falls. Trembles with her energy, though of course he's already dead.

Milena collapses, and her power recedes into her body.

The boy she saved touches her foot.

And I return to the battle.

Minutes later, I approach Milena. She's crying, alone.

I sit in front of her. "Are you OK?"

She shakes her head. "I killed someone. I've never killed anyone before. Except for Daniel, but that was an accident."

"You did what you had to do. That man would've killed the boy if you hadn't stopped him."

"Have you ever had to kill anyone?"

"Yes."

"Does it get easier?"

"The act is easier. But it's never easier to cope with afterward."

She weeps again, and I take her hands in mine.

Then a young woman dressed like a fairy approaches the corpse of the man Milena killed. The girl opens a pink bag. Pulls out a crayon. Kneels beside the body.

"What are you doing?" Milena says.

"Death is so ugly," the girl says. "I have to fix him."

"Don't touch him."

But the Beautifier only smiles and draws a light blue flower on the corpse's forehead. Milena turns away, and weeps again.

"Let's go home," I say. "I'll cook you breakfast."

She nods, squeezes my hands. Smiles.

Her heart is mine.

"Cailin," I say, because you're the first thought that comes to mind, but Milena doesn't awaken. Doesn't even stir.

She finally trusts me enough to let her guard down.

So now's the time to complete Phase Six.

Of course, the phantoms try to stop me. They freeze my flesh and scream in my skull. But ultimately, they lack any real power over me, because they're not Protectors. Not anymore.

I try not to look her in the face. Instead, I keep my gaze focused on her chest. And somehow, by limiting my perception, I can almost convince myself she's not a human being. She's just a bundle of flesh, no greater than the sum of her parts.

But the illusion won't give me the strength to proceed.

I need to hear your voice. I need to know you'll still want me, even after I accomplish my mission.

And then, finally, you say, through my lips, "I'll always love you."

And my conviction prevails, overshadowing my mercy once more.

"I'm sorry," I say, to Milena, to you. To myself.

Then my eyes dart about, out of control, and I'm no longer holding the sacred blade I picked up. This one's long, thin. Military issue. The same

Fungus of the Heart

kind the soldiers wielded when they stormed our hut and took you away. And I see your head on Milena's body.

But right now, I don't care.

Sometimes I need to do the right thing for love and be a villain.

So I kill Milena. Find the mushroom in her heart. Swallow.

I expect bitterness, because of her past, but her power tastes sweet. Kind.

Usually, after I devour a soul, the phantoms sob along with me. But I can't hear them as I mourn all the way to the Fortress.

And at the base of the mountain, I shudder, equally terrified and euphoric.

Very soon, I'll have the body to save you.

And we'll be together again, forever.

My courage peaks, and I summon the six mushrooms. And I wait, kneeling on the ground, eyes closed, lips trembling with your name. I feel my body tingling. And in few moments, I'll become much more of a monster than I already am.

Stronger. Bigger. More grotesque.

I hope you'll learn to love this nightmare. But even if you don't, I'll never let you go.

A heartbeat later, the spirits of the mushrooms rupture, and the energy thrashes my organs from within, and I squeal with the power and the pain.

Then, nothing.

The torture stops, and I don't change.

I feel like a prisoner taking that first step out of prison.

And maybe I misinterpreted Billy's messages. Maybe the dragon he showed me symbolizes my delusion. I see a dragon in the stone, the way I see a monster in my mind. Neither of them real. And maybe I'm the monkey in the spider's web, helpless, unable to conquer the Fortress. And maybe the broken key represents my inability to reach you. Not because you're trapped in the Fortress, but because you're dead.

And maybe it wasn't a coincidence that my mission required six mushrooms and the last stew I cooked for you also required six mushrooms.

I'm sorry, Cailin.

I called you an Imposter, but you only wanted to help me.

"Nightingale," you say, behind me.

But no, you're gone. And when I turn around, I see Milena. Only she's not a phantom like the others.

I reach out and touch her arm. Flesh and blood.

"Why did you leave?" she says.

My head whirls in chaos, but I manage to say, "Cailin."

"You should've told me you were leaving."

"I'm sorry."

She removes a smooth teal stone from her pocket. "I know you belong to Cailin, but I want you to have this. Even if you don't want to give me any part of you in return."

I take the soulstone and stare in her eyes.

This feels real.

Maybe I couldn't kill her, after all.

Maybe I didn't kill any of them.

But the phantoms swarm around me, emphasizing their deaths. So I mouth an apology for my doubt. I killed five Protectors, and maybe the phantoms will forgive me someday, but they'll never let me forget.

As I surrender a tear for those I murdered, a shadow thought seizes control of my mind.

I didn't complete Phase Six. And that's why I didn't grow into a nightmare. There's still a chance to save you.

No. You're dead.

"Are you listening to me?" Milena says, crossing her arms.

"I'm sorry," I say. "What were you saying?"

"I said I'll break her out for you. Cailin."

"You can't."

"And who's going to stop me? The soldiers?"

"You know what I mean. They can't harm you, so they'll go after your village instead."

"I don't care."

"You don't mean that."

"Well, you're right. But the soldiers capture or kill people just for being strong enough to oppose them. That's not right. And if they could overpower me, I'd be trapped in the Fortress too, like Cailin. Like so many others. I have the power to free them."

And of course, she's right.

And I want to tell her to go ahead.

Because maybe you're not really dead. Maybe you're trapped and frightened and alone, waiting for me to rescue you.

But if Milena enters the Fortress, she'll start a war.

And to win, she'll have to kill thousands of human beings. And maybe she'll convince herself that she's fighting for love, but she'll lose her soul, the way I lost mine.

And maybe I don't know what love means anymore.

But I'm going to do everything in my power to change back into the man you knew.

So I pocket the soulstone, and say, "Let's go home. I'll cook you breakfast."

And as Milena smiles, I'm that much closer to finding my heart.

Boy in the Cabinet

Live anywhere long enough, and eventually the space becomes a home. And maybe if I keep thinking at you hard enough, someday you'll become more than a Styrofoam cup. Maybe you'll sprout a brain, or at least a nerve cluster, and you'll hear me.

And when that happens, you won't confuse me or disagree with me all the time. You'll be an ideal companion, unlike a certain creature I know.

Speak of the feline devil. The Death Cat won't stop scratching the wood until I open the door, so I obey her command. "What do you want?"

Holly hacks up a ball of carnage onto the table. "Happy birthday, Boy."

"It's not my birthday."

"Yes, it is. I have a seventh sense for these things."

So I study the notches on the cabinet wall. Holly's right. Today's the anniversary of my life. Not to mention my mother's death and my father's transformation.

Trembling, I almost drop my mason jar filled with tears. "I told you last year. I don't celebrate birthdays."

"Well, I do." With her claws, the cat sifts through the wad of hair and clothes. "Here we go."

My eyes widen.

Holly licks the permanent marker clean, then sets the gift on my palms.

"You stole this from someone," I say. "Didn't you?"

The Death Cat washes her face with a paw. "It doesn't count as stealing if you eat the person first. Then the person's part of you, and you can't steal from yourself."

"Killing humans is even worse than stealing from them."

"I was hungry."

"That's not a good enough reason to murder somebody."

"So with a good enough reason, I'd be able to justify to you the killing of one of your kind?"

"Of course not. And maybe that proves what you're doing is wrong."

"Wrong for you, Boy. Not for me."

"How can you be so cruel?"

Holly sighs. "How many times do I have to tell you? I'm incapable of cruelty, because I don't empathize with my prey when I'm hunting them."

"You're a monster."

"Monsters don't have hearts. But me, I love my food. Just not the way you want me to."

"You shouldn't hurt the ones you love."

"Can't we agree to disagree?"

"No." I grab the doorknob. "Thanks for the present, cat."

"Wait, you—"

I close the door.

And by the light of my tiny sun, I draw you a smiley face and a prominent pair of ears.

Finally, you're real enough for a name. And while I've never met a Salvador, you definitely look like one.

"Can you hear me, Sal?"

My muscles ache with hope and the power of my birthday wish.

But you only grin in silence, a best friend waiting to happen.

Maybe next year.

Jeremy C. Shipp

Holly never visits after my sun burns out, so the scraping must be caused by some horrible fiend come to rape and pillage.

I imagine my body ripped in two, and I know I should embrace my fear.

But this fiend could be my father.

So I open the door.

"Holly," I say. Disappointed. Relieved.

"Hello, Boy." The Death Cat taps my chin with the top of her head.

"What are you doing here so late?"

Holly sits. "It's your birthday."

"Didn't we already have this conversation?" I try to sound sarcastic, but in truth, I'm not sure of the answer. My memories can be a little temperamental.

"Today's supposed to be special for you," the cat says. "You deserve more than a permanent marker."

"I'm sorry if I seemed ungrateful earlier. I really do like the gift."

"Whether you like the marker or not isn't the point. You deserve more. You need more. More than I could ever give you."

"If you can't help me, then what are you doing here?"

"I didn't say I was useless. I can still affect your choices."

"But you always say you don't like to involve yourself with the way other creatures live their lives."

"That's true. But you're not living. Not really."

I check my pulse, just to make sure. "You don't know what you're talking about."

"No, you don't know what I'm talking about. There's a difference."

"Then what are you talking about?"

"You need to get out of the cabinet."

Fungus of the Heart

I laugh, for the first time in ages. "But I'm the Boy in the Cabinet. If I leave here, I'll cease to exist."

"Or you'll change."

"That's even worse."

"Transmogrification can be a good thing."

"Tell that to my father."

The Death Cat touches my leg with her paw. "I understand your reservations, and I can't promise you that you'll live happily ever after in the world outside. But I can assure you that there's nothing worse than a wasted heart."

"I'm not wasting anything." And I hold you in front of the cat's face.

"That's a Styrofoam cup."

"For now."

Holly sighs. "You can't create life on your own, Boy."

"What do you know about life? You're just a stupid Death Cat."

"Death isn't separate from life."

I almost laugh again, but the swell of sorrow in my throat prevents me. "If that's true, then where's my mother? Why isn't she here?"

"No matter what I say, you're not going to believe the truth about death until you die. So we might as well drop the subject and move on."

"Fine. But you should know, you're not going to talk me into leaving here. Every word you say makes me want to throw up."

"Then I've failed you."

"Yes. You have."

I slam the door, and my jars clink together. And I hold on to my fury for as long as possible, but the feeling soon dies away. Because in spite of what happened to my mother, I don't hate Holly. I don't know how.

So I create a crack in my door, and find the cat curled up and crying.

"What's wrong?" I say.

"I want to help you," she says. "But I don't think I can. I'm sorry."

"Sorry? But I thought you can't feel any empathy."

"I never said that."

And as the cat continues to weep for me, a haze of faith spreads through my mind and clouds my thoughts.

Maybe she really cares about me.

Maybe I need to escape this place.

"You're trying to trick me," I say. "As soon as I leave the cabinet, you'll eat me."

Holly unfurls herself and looks at me with sparkling eyes. "If I was meant to eat you, do you really believe the cabinet could protect you?"

"Yes."

"Just because you feel safe somewhere doesn't mean you are."

I clutch you close to my chest. "I don't believe you."

"I'm afraid your beliefs don't have the power to shape this aspect of your reality. Sooner or later, death will find you in the cabinet."

"How?"

"I'm not destined to eat you, so I don't know. Maybe a monster or another Death Cat. Of course, if you survive long enough, your food and water jars will eventually run out."

I examine my supply with frantic eyes. "But they've never run out before."

"Be that as it may, only love can last forever."

Once again, the stupid Death Cat's ravaged my mind beyond recognition. And I can't seem to think the same thoughts anymore.

I don't want to die.

But if that's my only choice, I want to die with love in my heart.

And for the first time in my short life, the cabinet feels too small.

So I say, "How do I do it? How do I leave the cabinet?"

"Well," the cat says. "You step out."

The concept seems more than a little ridiculous, but I follow her direction anyway.

And in an instant, I find myself on the table.

And I collapse, shaking all over.

Holly curls up beside me. "I know you feel especially vulnerable, but you're in just as much danger as you always were."

"That's supposed to make me feel better?" I say.

"Hmm. Good point. Pet me, and I'll give you some of my strength."

I don't hesitate.

And as she purrs, my body warms and tingles.

"That's enough," she says.

So I remove my hand. "What do I do now?"

"Move on."

I scan the hundreds of exits in the room. "But which door is the right one?"

"You shouldn't think that way, Boy. Just pick a door and walk out."

"But what if I hate where I end up? I'm not like you. When I leave this place, I won't be able to return again."

"True. But if you become consumed by your power of choice, you'll never leave."

"Will you choose for me?"

"No."

I feel the urge to close myself off again, so I face my cabinet. But instead of climbing inside, I grab a jar of piss and shit.

And with this weapon in one hand, and my jar of tears in the other, I approach a simple wooden door that reminds me of home.

Then I face the Death Cat once more.

I'm not sure if I want to thank her or curse her.

But in the end, I say, "Thank you, Holly."

"You're welcome," she says, still too weak to sit up. "I hope you die a wonderful death."

"You too."

And with that, I touch the doorknob.

I imagine a life of monsters and misery on the other side, and part of me wants to embrace my fear.

But this path could lead me to love.

So I open the door.

The wide, wide world pulls at me from every direction, and if not for the thorny bush rooting me to the ground, I'm sure I would ascend into the azure abyss above.

I hate this place already.

And this place obviously hates me back.

But a drop of optimism dilutes my terror as soon as a girl in green appears atop a boulder.

"How do you do that?" I say.

She jumps and lands in front of me. "Do what?"

"Not fly."

"That's easy. I just don't become a bird."

"Is it common for children to become birds?"

"Not common at all, I'm afraid. I'd love to fly. At least for a few days of the year."

"Why?"

She gazes up at the horrible blue void. "The sky's beautiful. Don't you think?"

I try to imitate her warm expression, but I can't see through her eyes. "I don't like the sky."

"Don't worry. You will someday." She touches my arm.

And in that moment, I release my grip on the shrub.

And I don't soar to my death.

So I pick up my weapon once more, but the jar of excrement slips from my bloody hand. "Shit!"

"What is that?" the girl says.

"Porridge. Are there many monsters around here?"

"It doesn't smell like porridge."

"Never mind that. What about the monsters?"

"I'm the Girl Who Monsters Fear." She takes my hand. "I'll protect you."

I believe her.

And for some strange reason, I want to run at her as fast as I can. I want to smash into her, and jumble pieces of me with pieces of her.

Maybe she's a wife waiting to happen.

But I don't want to make my father's mistake. He fell in love with the Woman Who Can't Bear Children, in spite of her mortality. And he suffered the consequences.

The day I came into being, my mother ceased to exist.

And one day, a monster will refuse to fear the Girl Who Monsters Fear, and she'll probably disappear too.

In the end, I need to find a partner I can't love to help me create life.

So I release the girl's hand, and escape the trap.

The door I knock on tonight looks almost exactly like the door I passed through to enter this world.

Or maybe not. My memories like to play with me sometimes.

But I'm not in the mood for games.

So I ignore the door and focus on the man.

"I'm sorry to bother you, sir," I say. "But I'm tired and hungry. I haven't eaten for days."

The man shrugs. "I couldn't care less."

"You couldn't?"

"No."

I smile. "Are you in need of a servant? I'd be happy to work for food and shelter."

The man rubs his beard, then opens the door wide.

I follow him inside.

His home would remind me of every other home in the area, if not for the pyramid of stacked excrement jars.

"What can I do for you?" I say.

He motions to the far wall. "Everyone in the world wants to live inside my cabinet, but I hate when people stay in there. So I need you to stay in there and stand guard."

"But if you hate when people go in there, won't you hate when I go in there?"

"No."

"Why?"

"Because you don't count."

"Why not?"

The man sighs. "It's a complicated issue. And on my list of things I hate, complicated issues are ranked fourteen. That's fourteen out of six thousand and twenty seven. So you can understand my reluctance to answer your question."

"Of course."

"So you'll take the job?"

I nod.

And the man forces me into the cabinet, closes the door, and locks me in.

I'm home again.

Sometimes, the Man Who Can't Smile allows me to join him for dinner, but I don't think he yearns for my company the way I yearn for yours. I

Fungus of the Heart

think he likes to watch me enjoy my meal the way he can't anymore.

But the dinners never end well, because he can't taste through my mouth, no matter how hard he tries.

So like always, he knocks over the table, and says, "Get back in the cabinet, Boy."

I don't. "I'm not going to help you anymore, unless you help me bring Salvador to life."

"Who's Salvador?"

I pull you out of my pouch.

And the Man scoffs. "What a stupid-looking cup."

"He's not stupid," I say.

"I didn't say he's stupid. I said he's stupid-looking. Although I'm sure he's as stupid as he looks."

You don't deserve this, so I try to cover your ears.

But the Man snatches you away from me.

"Give him back!" I say.

The Man throws you on the floor, and grabs me by the arms. He forces me back into the cabinet.

"Let me out!" I say.

He doesn't.

And through the keyhole, I watch him drink from you as if he owns you.

Now, I'm sure.

I'm going to die in here. Unloved. Alone.

You have to understand.

Normally, I wouldn't try to kill another person, but I don't think this thing counts as one.

I'm almost positive.

So I say, "Have you heard the one about the decapitated mouse and the talking intestines?"

The Man shakes his head.

So I tell him the only joke I know, but the Man doesn't seem to appreciate Death Cat humor, because he doesn't even smirk once.

I sigh.

Then I notice the notches on the cabinet wall.

"It's my birthday," I say.

"So?" the Man says.

"I want to hold Sal."

And my muscles ache with hope and the power of my birthday wish.

Finally, the Man says, "It's my birthday too. Therefore, my wish cancels out your wish. You get nothing."

I want to cry, but my mason jar can't hold any more tears.

So I watch in silence as the man pours hot water into you.

Then, after all my years of waiting for you, you scream.

And I want so much to hold you in my arms.

"It hurts!" you say.

And I know what it's like to burn, because a strange fire always flares up in my face whenever I think about what happened to my parents.

"Help me!" you say. "Help me!"

I realize now that you're more than my friend.

And of course I want to save you, but I don't want to face the Man outside. I recognize him now. I recognize myself in him. And if I leave this cabinet, I'll probably end up becoming him.

I'm better off locked up. If I ignore your pleas and my heart long enough, all my suppressed emotions will transform me. And become me. And in this state, I'll never feel anything ever again.

I imagine myself as a monster, and part of me wants to embrace a life without fear.

But I love you enough to love myself.
So I kick open the door. Easily.
And I say, "Pour out the water."
"Never," the Man says.
"I'll fight you if I have to."
"You don't stand a chance."
"I don't?"
"You're a Child. I'm a Man."

I feel the urge to close myself off again, so I face my cabinet. But instead of climbing inside, I reach for a container of piss and shit.

Then I change my mind.

So I throw my jar of suffering at the Man's face.

And he bleeds and shrinks and cries my tears.

And maybe he feels happy for me, because he smiles too, even when Holly pounces from the shadows and rips him apart.

And in the Man's place comes the Man With a Cup for a Son.

So I dump out the hot water, and fill you with love.

Just Another Vampire Story

When She Found Out

Steven had hoped for a fight the day Helena found out.

He imagined the episode quite often. She would toss his clothes out the window, like in all the movies. And he would say something like, "Please! Let's talk about this like adults!" At some point in the heat of it all she would smack him in the face with a memento of their lives together. Say, a framed photograph or one of those frowning porcelain clowns he'd always bought her for her birthday.

He'd touch his face and feel the liquid come forth. Yes, some blood would be nice. The crimson streams running down his nose and trickling along the crevice of his lips. So that he could just barely taste it.

But Steven had no such luck.

Helena simply met him at the door and whispered in a drawn out breath, "You cheated on me." She locked herself in the bathroom. And wouldn't come out. And wouldn't speak. And Steven scrubbed the kitchen floor because he didn't know how to clean away the darkness he'd shoved into Helena's heart.

When She Rocked

Steven wasn't sure, but he suspected that Helena had slept in the bathtub all night. When he saw her the next morning, she walked with the stiffness of a door. A closed, knob-less door Steven could no longer open.

She didn't look at him. She didn't eat the food he offered. Steven spoke but he doubted she heard a word.

All she did was rock. Back and forth on their bed, spawning little squeaks that kept the time. She stared through him, through the walls, to a place where Steven couldn't touch her.

God, what had he done? Why? It was the only thing she'd ever really asked of him. He knew she had been victimized her whole life. Parents, friends, boyfriends, strangers. There was a bull's-eye etched somewhere into her skin. Or maybe it was her eyes.

He couldn't comprehend why he'd sacrificed so much for a few measly hours of pleasure with Mary the Secretary.

The only explanation he could muster was that he'd been drawn to her. By some force out of his control.

When She Spoke

"Do you hear it, Steven?"

Steven almost burst into tears at the sound of her voice. He fell to his knees before her and said, "The TV's on in the other room. I'll turn it off if it's bothering you."

"No. Not that. Not that."

"What is it then?"

"The drums."

"I don't—"

"Thousands of them, beating all at once. Bum...bum...bum..." She rocked with the rhythm of her voice.

"The only beating I hear is from my own heart." Maybe too soap opera, but he was getting desperate. "Please talk to me. Do you hate me now? Do you want me to leave? Give me something."

"Do whatever you want, Steven."

"What I want is to help you feel better."

"I'm fine. The drums are enough."

This was getting him nowhere. And it hurt too much. He stood and headed for the door.

"Steven."

He spun. "Yeah?"

"They're getting louder."

When She Left

She crept out from their bedroom in the middle of the night. As she passed the couch in the living room, Steven pretended to be fast asleep. He even snored a little. It took a lot of willpower to keep himself from grinning.

Yes, maybe she had finally come to her senses. She was going out to cheat on him. Of course she was. He had to follow. The pain of watching her with another man would surely drain away some of the guilt pounding through his veins.

She took her truck. He, his.

Thirty minutes later, Steven found himself trekking through the forest, swerving feverishly to avoid the trees.

Perhaps she knew he was following. Perhaps not. Perhaps it didn't matter.

When She Changed

He followed her into the cave. A potent musk stung at his nostrils, and it only got worse the farther they went. It smelled like a marriage between dead skunk and wet dog.

Steven's body collapsed to cold ground when his eyes spotted them. But as quickly as he fell, he brought himself back up. He had to.

They numbered a hundred or so, bunched together, interspersed at equal distances. Nude, muscular—not like bodybuilders, more like… gorillas—wide-eyed, like Japanese cartoon characters…human.

They swayed constantly, without any perceivable purpose. And yet, there was a synchronism to their movements. As if invisible strings pinned to their arms and legs, linked one to the next, spawning an intricate web of harmonic motion.

Helena approached them. As soon as she was in reach, they ripped off her clothes and tossed each article behind them, far into the darkness. He could only see the back of her now.

One of the creatures, the cantor, the one the others seemed to swarm around, was the only to clutch a torch. He neared Helena with closed eyes. He smiled at her.

"Helena," said the cantor melodically. The crowd jerked with every syllable. "I am glad you finally opened your ears to the rhythm. Do you wish to join the choir?"

She nodded. A single, forceful nod that brought Steven to his knees.

Gently, he tilted her head to the side, leaned forward, and dug his teeth into her neck. It only lasted a moment. He released her. She collapsed to the ground.

Steven wanted to run to her. To pull her to safety. But when he saw the smile on her face—that smile he had brought to dusk with his stupidity—he stood motionless.

The cantor helped her up. She stood by him, swaying now, the same as the others.

The grin never left her face. Even as they, one after another, took turns drinking from the river of blood that ran down her pale skin.

When She Was Gone

Steven scrubbed the kitchen floor. Every day. Sometimes more.

Sometimes, he would see Helena in the polished reflection.

She looked up at him from another world. He never lifted his eyes to see if she really was standing beside him. He knew she wasn't. He also knew she wasn't angry. The look in her eyes made that perfectly clear.

Those eyes said, "I'm sorry, Steven. I was drawn to them. And there was nothing I could do."

Ticketyboo

When Flowers Die

There was no trail through the field of flowers, so Jill made her own. Those she trampled on the first day were trampled on every other day until they died. Jill felt bad for the poor little things she sacrificed, but it was the best way.

Jill liked staring at the field at night. Much better than the stars, because the flowers were illuminated with color. Blues and purples and reds. She watched them waltz with the sky and for a few moments she could forget what had brought her here to Ticketyboo.

Jeff tugged on her dress with stubby fingers and shattered her mellow thoughts into coarse shards. "Jill, I wanna pick flowers for Mommy."

"Mommy..." Jill trembled. She inhaled deeply and allowed the fragrance in the air to tickle her nostrils. This calmed her nerves. "Mommy's gone." Blood. Glass. Fire. "You remember what happened...don't you?"

"No, not that one. New mommy."

"She's not our Mommy!" Jill erupted. The entire meadow seemed to dance wildly from the force of her outburst. But it was just the wind, she knew.

Jeff scrunched up his face and when his muscles finally relaxed, tears came forth. They sprinted down his peppermint cheeks.

"I'm sorry," she said and patted him on the head. "Let's get some flowers for Martha." They went to work collecting the brightest, most beautiful flowers they could find.

"Jill, why do they scream when we pull them out?" Jeff cringed every time he heard their tiny squeaks.

Jill didn't. "It only hurts them for a second, then they're okay. You shouldn't worry about them."

Jeff nodded and smiled just a little.

When Flowers Burn

"These are for me?" Martha took the bouquet and pressed it close to her naked chest. The thorns of the roses dug into her flesh, but she didn't seem to mind. Jill watched the little rivers of blood travel down Martha's pale skin and fall onto the glass floor. Drip. Drop.

Jill wondered if it had always been like this—glass walls, glass ceiling, glass furniture, glass everything—or if it was a result of Martha's cleaning habits. Martha spent most of her day polishing, washing. Perhaps she'd washed her clothes into nothingness, polished her home into a colorless mass.

"Now," said Martha. "Let's watch them die." And she used a crystal match to light them on fire. The petals radiated brighter and brighter until they burst, all at once, creating a cloud of teal dust that sparkled in the air.

Jeff clapped his hands with excitement. Jill was a little too old for that kind of response, so she simply smiled.

The stems of the flowers burned next. Little fingers of cerise smoke reached out and shoved themselves up Jill's nose. She had never smelled burning flowers before. It was nice. Like fresh cherry pie. It almost made her forget she wanted to kill people.

Sick Dog

To get to the one and only restaurant of Ticketyboo, they had to walk a road of shiny blue gravel that matched the sky. Clusters of white pebbles rolled together in sync with the clouds above. During the night Jill knew all the rocks, except the smallest white ones, would bury themselves under the earth. Then those remaining would reflect the stars and moon and the occasional shooting star.

Martha and the other caregivers never ate or spoke in the restaurant. They seemed content watching the children gobble up the only food available: sweet sponges that they didn't really eat, but sucked on and swallowed. Jill loved the sponges when she first came to Ticketyboo, but then she remembered the way her father adored cigarettes and how hard he worked to quit because he didn't want to die. Jill didn't know what the sponges were doing to her so every day she ate less and less and less until she overcame the craving completely.

Jill pretended to eat her sponges and sneaked them into the napkin on her lap.

The sounds and smells of cheerful vomiting saturated the air around her. Like a mosaic of fountains, the children spewed all over the elegant glass chamber. The sponges went in bright and colorful and came out black and mucusy and stunk like gasoline. During it all, the children grinned because it tasted as good coming up as it did going down. She remembered how they used to feel traveling through her body. Wriggling around like they were washing her from the inside.

Jill faked throwing up under the table and watched Sick Dog as he scampered about and licked the mounds of upchuck off the floor. Sick Dog didn't look sick really, in fact he wagged his tail all the time. But Jill always imagined what his insides must've looked like eating what he did. Whatever it was.

Tuck

"This is a special day for the both of you." Martha sat on the chair between Jill's bed and Jeff's. She held two wrapped presents—see-though, like everything else, and yet the gifts inside were invisible. Just two boxes filled with nothing but air, it seemed. "These are for you."

Fungus of the Heart

"It's not my birthday." Jill crossed her arms. "It's not Jeff's either."

"I know." Martha placed the gifts on their laps. "Today is special for another reason. It has been exactly one year since the incident. Since I became your guardian. These gifts are not meant to celebrate what happened that day. Certainly not. Only to symbolize your progress. I am so proud of you both. You know that, yes?"

"Yes," Jeff replied.

Jill shrugged.

"Well...open them." Martha clasped her hands together and grinned.

Even after the year she spent with Martha, Jill wasn't sure she trusted Martha's smiles. They seemed sincere enough. As honest and naked as her body, but there was just something about the way she revolved around Jill and her brother. All of the other adults Jill knew had better things to do than read their children stories, watch them as they played, clean the house so that everything was clear and never scary. Martha seemed to know perfectly well that both Jill and her brother believed in monsters. Why else would she make the house impossible to hide in?

Jill appreciated all that but she still thought Martha was strange. No husband, no job, no pets. Her life was the children.

"Come on, Jill," Jeff said, ripping open his gift.

Although she gave no commands to her body to do so, her hands clawed at the crystal paper, revealing a colored box inside. She hadn't been able to see the color through the gift-wrapping. And Jill didn't like that.

Her gift was exactly the same as Jeff's. Jack-in-the-boxes. Striped with blues and purples and reds. The box strained her eyes—no, hurt them. She wasn't used to such boundaries in Martha's house. Nothing was hidden here. She didn't have to pull a drawer open to know exactly what was inside.

But this box. This stupid little box hid its contests from Jill. She joined Jeff in twirling the handle around and around. The music wasn't music at all. It was her parents. Crying. The sound burrowed into Jill's eyes and made them close, tight. Tears began to seep out.

She heard Jeff's box burst open.

Jill immediately forced her eyes open and swiveled her head to see what Jack looked like. But Jill saw no Jack.

Jeff was staring at his box with a smile. "Thank you, Momm...Martha."

"I thought you would like it," Martha responded.

"Let me see," Jill said. Jeff handed the box over and she looked inside. Nothing but darkness. "Do you see something, Jeff?"

"Don't you see?" was his reply.

"I...I don't know. I don't think so. What does Jack look like?"

"Sad."

Jill returned the box and went to work on her own. Every turn singed her tummy with pain. She didn't want to hear her parents cry, but she didn't want to stop until Jack came out. But he just wouldn't.

"Mine won't come out, Martha," Jill complained. "It's broken."

"No, Jill. It is not." She took a deep breath. "It is time for bed now. You can play with your gifts more tomorrow."

"But Martha..." Jill started.

"I am sorry, but you need your rest. Tomorrow, Jill, you and I will go to the Shack again."

Jill's stomach went inside out. "I don't want to go."

"I know." Martha tucked them both in tight and left.

Jill felt cocooned by the quilt, even if it was transparent. Warm, but tight. Maybe too tight. She wondered if she could get out if she wanted to. Better not to try. Not to know.

Overzealous Cuticles

Nightmares didn't last long in Ticketyboo. At least not without a conscious effort to keep the dark things from turning into dead things. It was the Big Hand that reached into Jill's mind and changed her dreams. If a monster chased her, the hand plunged into the beast's throat and yanked out its bones so the flesh collapsed like a deflated balloon.

Fungus of the Heart

There were no dark corners in Jill's nightmares tonight though. She sat under an umbrella in a vast desert and drank lemonade. It hadn't taken long for her to realize that these monsters were part of her mind. The shadows had tried to keep that information from her, to cram her with fear. But she'd destroyed the darkness and nothing was scary anymore. The monsters were under her control now and she redirected their rage toward the Big Hand. She didn't hate the Big Hand, but the rage had to go somewhere.

The hand worked with a frantic fury. It decapitated a vampire with its sharpened fingernail, squished a werewolf between two fingers (Jill watched the guts ooze out like a bloody furball and yawned), and flicked a moaning zombie into the sun. Jill wondered how long it could keep fighting like this against an endless supply of monsters, covered with protruding veins, cuts and bruises. The hand had been so strained lately it didn't even take care of itself properly anymore, with hangnails and overzealous cuticles.

Jill took another sip of her lemonade and didn't even mind the eyeballs floating in her glass, the juices of which made her lemonade pink.

Bound in White

The Shack was made of frozen milk. Not cold, just frozen in time. Solidified. It made the air stink like too much melted butter.

Jill sat in the center of this whiteness, strapped to a chair. The first couple months she had struggled, but soon accepted the fact that the effort was futile. And there was no point in closing her eyes. Martha had washed them too many times, and her eyelids were clear now. So she had to watch it. Over and over.

The milky waterfall spewed down from a slit in the roof, swallowed up by a hole in the ground. Something made the images appear on the waterfall, but Jill wasn't sure what. Maybe they projected right out of her eyes.

Jeremy C. Shipp

It wasn't easy watching the images. To see her parents bleed and scream and cry. Sure, there was some sadness, and Jill savored that feeling. But inside there was also something else. Little claws that clenched her stomach and twisted it around. And tiny volcanoes under her skin that burned her from the inside out until she felt like there were too many blankets wrapped around her.

Hatred. She wanted the bad men who hurt her parents to suffer. She didn't like hating so much...

Oh, to be a little girl again. To be able to jump rope without remembering the girls playing on the sidewalk who were splattered with blood, and got all their pretty dresses dirty.

In order to avoid some of the rage from escaping the little black box she'd built inside her heart, she tried to pay attention to the details. Like the kitty with a black spot on his nose that was walking on the fence...and when he heard the gunshot all the hairs on his back stood up like a comb. Or the yellow butterfly with black spots that danced past the smoke that flew up into the clouds from the crashed car with bullet holes in its windows. Or the pool of blood on the asphalt shaped like an elephant. Or—

"How do you feel?" Martha asked, unstrapping her from behind.

The milky waterfall stopped flowing and that made tears come out of Jill's eyes. "Martha, you made me stay here too long this time. It never lasted this long before."

"How do you feel?" she repeated in the same sunny tone.

"Bad."

"Angry?"

Jill realized something at that moment. This exact dialogue had occurred every other time she'd been to the Shack. How do you feel? Bad. Angry? Yes. And that was that. Jill was tired of it. So this time she responded, "No. Not angry."

"Are you sad, Jill?"

"Yes. I'm sad."

"I'm glad."

Bad Men Must Die

Jill awoke in the middle of the night because she felt frozen. Blues and purples and reds filled her vision. The flower field. She was outside.

One of the bad men towered over her. Smiling. His clothes were baggy, too big for his body, just like before. Like he was trying to hide a skeleton underneath. Trying to be big when he was really small.

Jill remembered what he did to her parents. She remembered their tears.

"I hate you! I hate you!" She grabbed his gun. The weight of the thing made her collapse onto her behind. The bad man didn't do anything. He just stayed still and stared with that skeleton grin.

She raised the gun as high as she could and fired. The gun flew right out of her hands and she scrambled after it. When she looked back at the bad man, she saw that his shin was bleeding. He stood there like a flamingo for a moment before he tumbled over.

The fire inside her made her walk onto his stomach and jump up and down. Every time she landed on him his lips made funny shapes. Always a little different. Then she knelt down on him and bashed his chest with the handle of the gun. She kept doing it until she heard something crack. The sound kept going even after she stopped hitting him.

She remembered the look on her mother's face.
She pointed the gun at the bad man's left eye. More than anything else she wanted to fire. He deserved to—

Wait...

No. This wasn't him. A real bad man would fight back. A real bad man would take the gun and shoot her in the eye. And then shoot her in the other eye even though she would already be dead.

Jill dropped the gun onto a purple flower, which crushed it.

"You did it, Jill," the bad man said, in Martha's voice. "You beat it. You beat it."

Jill quickly rolled off of the bad man's body.

"I am so proud of you," he said. "My sweet, sweet Jill."

Going Home

Jill rushed into the living room and found Martha polishing the floor. Martha always did the floors first thing in the morning.

"Martha! Martha! Look!"

"What is it, Jill?"

Jill held out the jack-in-the-box, grinning. It was wide open. "I did it! I did it!"

"You did. I knew you would." Martha arose and touched Jill's cheek. "You see now? Your parents are sad, but they are okay. The bad men did not kill them too. They are together."

"I see it." Jill stared into the box.

"This has worked out wonderfully. Now you and Jeff may return to the world together. You are both ready. Jeff! Come here, my dear!"

Jeff made his way down the stairs, drowsily, picking the sleep out of his eyes. "What is it, Mommy?"

"I am not your mommy, Jeff," Martha said, to Jill's satisfaction. "I am glad you think so highly of me though. I called you because I have good news. You can go back now. Both of you. Together."

"Where?" Jeff asked.

"To the world. You can see your mommy and your daddy again. You can see whatever you want to see, and go wherever you want to go. You can talk to your grandmother. The one who died. And no one will ever hurt you ever again."

"Not even the bad men?" he said.

"Not even them."

Jeff smiled.

Jill smiled too, but she wasn't thinking about her grandmother or even her parents.

"Goodbye, Jeff. Goodbye, Jill." She hugged them both, pressing her naked breasts against their cheeks. "You are good children." A tear strolled down the side of her pale nose and plopped onto the part of the floor she'd been polishing.

Martha pointed at Jeff and he disappeared. Then she pointed at Jill.

Jill now understood the reason she and her brother were sent to Ticketyboo after they died. Because Martha and her friends were afraid Jeff and Jill would haunt the bad men for making their parents cry so much. The word haunt did not do justice to what Jill was capable of. Adults without good imaginations would haunt. Jill wanted to torture them and make them suffer in ways no one ever had before.

She felt herself being swept away. Soon she would be at the world again, and she could do whatever she wanted to the bad men.

Martha was so stupid. Maybe she'd figure it out someday though. Maybe she'd be gardening in the field. And she'd dig up Jill's jack-in-the-box. The one that never opened.

The Escapist

Maybe my sense of humor's a bit darker than usual, but torture can do that to a person. So when the drunken bards gush with masturbatory music about The Escapist's numerous exploits and destinies, I tell them they forgot a verse.

And I sing:

He betrayed his soul for turnip bread,

Every chance he got.

He even gave the Goblins head,

Without a second thought.

The bard closest to me points his flute at my heart, and says, "Hold your tongue, you...giant."

"That's the best you can come up with?" I say. "I'm barely taller than you are."

A much shorter musician gets in my face and says, "The Escapist is a hero, boy."

"You don't know anything about him," I say.

"I know he escaped the Farm. And no one escapes the Farm. He's gonna help us end this war."

"Even if the Escapist was the Gnome of your ballads, he couldn't stop the Goblins. No one can. We're fucked."

At this point, my escort returns from the latrine, and says, "Sorry for the delay, sir. Must've eaten a bad mushroom this morning."

Fungus of the Heart

"How horrible for you," I say, stabbing at his ears with sarcasm. Because only days ago, I would've killed for the most malicious of fungi.

"Thank you, sir. We'd best move on now. The General's eager to finally meet you. Lately, he's spoken of little else."

I tell him to lead the way.

But instead of following the soldier, I watch the eyes of the bards. I wait for the moment. I hold my breath.

Then the truth smacks them hard.

"You're not the Escapist," one of them says. Insists.

"You're too young," says another.

The other one just drops her drum.

Maybe I orchestrated all this to cheer myself up, but the looks on their faces don't bless me with a single chuckle.

The problem, I suppose, is that this isn't one of my plays. And the irony of my cruelty doesn't outweigh the fact that these are real Gnomes, with real feelings.

"Is he really the one?" someone asks. It doesn't matter who.

My escort nods, smiling like he's proud. Like he's my father.

And as the last of the hope drains from the wasted crowd, a jagged clump of empathy twists in my gut.

Of course, this doesn't stop me from loathing these fools for their ignorance.

Their innocence.

They cloud their minds with lyrical delusions, and they see war when there's only slaughter. They see heroes when there's only me. And they see a future when there's none to be had.

Still, the plastered lute player was right about one thing.

No one escapes the Farm.

Because even though my body's walking and talking here, my spirit's back there in the cage. Curled up on the floor. Begging for mercy.

Torture can do that to a person.

Jeremy C. Shipp

One heartbeat in the hut, and I can already tell General Torrent expects me to save the world.

Sure, his face looks stoic enough. But I can see the childlike excitement in his deformed wing. There, he can't stop himself from twitching.

"Well done, Swan," the General says to my escort. "Once again you've proven yourself a better Gnome than I. Double rations for you tonight."

"Thank you, sir," Swan says.

After the soldier leaves, the General motions for me to join him on his blanket.

It's not polite to refuse his offer, of course, so that's what I do.

The General grins.

Then, he says, "Who were you?"

"Were?" I say.

"I may be a Riversoul, but I'm smart enough to know that you're no longer the Gnome you used to be. I'm asking you who you were before they took him from you."

Suddenly, I'm bursting with respect for this stranger.

And I'm not one of his soldiers, but I already want to die for him.

Or maybe I just want to die.

"My name was Feather Thundersoul," I say, sitting.

"The young playwright?" the General says.

"That's the one."

"Before falling from grace, I was lucky enough to attend one of your plays. And I must admit, I'm quite a fan. Even with this war haunting my skull, many of your words remain with me."

And I can't help but smile, like I'm proud. Like I'm still Feather Thundersoul.

Fungus of the Heart

"Forgive my manners," the General says. "Can I get you something to eat? Drink?"

I'm hungry and thirsty, but I shake my head.

"Can I get you anything else?' he says. "The last I heard, you were female. Has your status changed, or did the Goblins deny you your choice of gender?"

I want to lie.

I want to hide my foul desire to be female behind my beard.

But to remain male would mean shouting silent soliloquies to the world.

"I'm not looking for a mate," my features would say. "Because I don't need anyone right now. Because I'm happy with myself."

The thought overwhelms me with nausea.

"They wouldn't let me shave," I say. "They knew I would've killed myself with the razor."

"Of course," the General says, standing. "Shall I shave you then?"

"OK," I say, before the other part of me has time to say no.

The General's wing spasms.

Soon, I'm soaking my chin in a basin of warm water. And General Torrent whistles, honing and stropping his razor.

I can't help but remember the first time my fathers shaved me, because they whistled too. Back then, my yearning to abandon childhood was more than a little confusing to me, but my fathers shined and kissed my naked cheeks. Made me feel proud of my womanhood.

Now, General Torrent's rubbing Aloe on my skin, searching my eyes for a savior, I'm sure.

I want to tell him the truth.

I want to disappoint him now, and get the hard part over with.

But I close my eyes instead.

Soon, his blade caresses my face. And I feel cared for, and special. And maybe this is all a manipulation to get me to open up and spill my guts.

But I don't care.

At least he's using kindness instead of the alternative.

Afterward, he leans over and kisses my cheek, like he's a family member or a friend. And I let him.

He shows me my reflection in a sword, and says, "Adequate?"

I nod.

I almost thank him.

"Now," General Torrent says. "Why don't you tell me everything you remember."

"Alright," I say.

And I give him most of the details, but I don't tell him everything. I don't tell him that when I was trapped, all I could think about was going home. But now that I'm free, the thought of returning to the Yard makes me want to puke my heart out.

I can't face them.

They'd see a relative, a friend, when there's only a walking, talking scar.

I finish the story of my so-called escape.

"Is there anything else?" the General says.

"No," I say.

And once again, General Torrent can't hide his true feelings from me, as his wing droops with disappointment and despair. He is ashamed of me, of course. But even more than that, he hates himself for believing in me.

Still, the General says, "I'm sure this information will prove invaluable to the cause."

"Right," I say.

"This may be too much to ask, but in my role, I'm often disallowed the luxury of courtesy. So I beseech you, cousin. Would you postpone your journey home to remain in our hutment for the time being? I'll have more questions for you in the days to come."

And, naturally, what he's really saying is, "Could you help me to create an illusion of progress in order to bolster morale?"

I can't help them win the war. But I do know something about putting on a show.

So I say, "Sure."

General Torrent invites me to the battlefield the same way he invites me to tea. With a grin, and a look of tenderness in his eyes.

And, once again, I accept.

Swan sits beside me, on the branch. Just in case a Goblin decides to climb the tree and slay me.

Of course, this won't happen.

The Goblins are too busy being slaughtered.

"Why don't they have a fighter with them?" I say.

And Swan says, "Lucky for us, sir, not all Goblins can afford bodyguards. General says the economic stratification of Gob society is one of the few weak points we can exploit."

"Ah."

The brutality I faced at the Farm felt so real. Too real. But now, looking down on the violence below, I feel detached. Numb.

I watch as the circle of Gnomes overpower the parents, and close in on the Goblin youngling.

"What's the point of killing them?" I say.

"What do you mean, sir?" Swan says.

"They're obviously not Farmers. What good can come from this?"

"General says this is a war of societies. Maybe these Gobs don't work at the Farm, but they eat the Gnomes kept there. They're part of the system. And any affront to that system will benefit our cause."

"I see."

My forehead's starting to throb, and I blame the thoughts clustering in my head. So I focus on the battle again.

Like General Torrent, many of the Gnomes aren't quite natural bodied. They have shells, claws, scales.

One soldier has a horn jutting out of his eye socket.

Another has a fox head for a hand.

And I say, "I'm surprised you managed to recruit conjurers into your army. The Stonesouls seemed bent on never leaving the Yard, back when I was living there."

"The Stonesouls remain as stubborn as ever, sir. They refuse to fight with us."

"Then who's doing the conjuring?"

"General says the creative minds of the Thundersouls are conducive to spellcasting. Given enough practice."

I should've guessed, but maybe I didn't want to believe the General could make such a reckless mistake.

There's no way a Thundersoul could ever properly invoke a spirit. This requires a stillness of mind, a quieting of inner demons that a Gnome like me could never achieve.

Believe me, I've tried.

Once again, my mind paints a dreamscape of the Farm. I see smears of blood, blurry faces. Sometimes I'm a prisoner. Sometimes I'm a guard.

Nothing makes sense anymore.

The nightworld used to barrage me with sanguine images that I channeled into my plays. Even in the worst of times, I gave the Yard hope. I insisted the meaning of life was home and love.

Fungus of the Heart

But now I know that everything's meaningless.

And the thunder of my soul is silenced.

So instead of writing my dreams into a notebook by my bed, I put on my hat, and follow the screams that woke me up.

The sound leads me to a hut on the outskirts of the encampment. A hut that most of the soldiers avoid altogether.

Of course, I have no doubt what manner of creature these shrieks belong to, as this sound has become commonplace to me in the past few weeks.

Sure enough, I find a Goblin in the hut. Tied to a post. His skin overgrown with boils and buds. The tips of the flowers drip with pus.

"What's wrong with you?" I say.

The Goblin strains against his ropes, and I can hear his boils popping.

Then he says, "I'll swallow you whole, you fucking grub!"

After wincing, I say, "How long have they kept you here?"

He screeches in pain again.

I survey the room, and see two blankets scattered with clay canisters and jars. Mortars and pestles. Beyond the blankets, there's an athanor.

"I'll drink every last drop of you!" the Goblin says.

Turning my head, I see myself tied to the post. I'm pleading for mercy.

"You'll kill me if I let you go," I say. Whisper.

And the Goblin says, "I'll devour you, and shit you onto your mother's fucking face!"

Someone touches my shoulder, and I'm sure another Goblin's come to finish me off. Finally.

"Forgive me," General Torrent says. "I'm the one to blame for disrupting your nightworld, as I've consistently failed in finding a gag that Number Twelve can't bite through."

"I'll butcher you and all your family," the Goblin says.

"That's far from polite, Number Twelve."

The Goblin stares at the ground.

"What's wrong with his skin?" I say.

"He's ill," the General says.

"I thought Goblins couldn't get sick."

"That is the common presumption, yes. But I never did hold much value to such sensational beliefs. Life is too fragile a thing to be so indomitable."

"Did you do this to him?"

"Physically, yes. I gave him this disease. However, if you're looking for the responsible party, you'll have to look at this tragedy in a more systemic light. The Goblins themselves…"

The General keeps talking, I'm sure, but I'm back in the Farm again. Coughing up blood.

I return to the hut when General Torrent pats my back.

And he says, "I understand your disgust. And I wish war didn't beget the need for horrible acts. In the end, all we can hope for is a quick resolution."

"Yeah," I say.

The General smiles. "Now if you'll excuse the interruption, I must ensure that our prisoner doesn't starve to death."

I watch the general as he removes an arm from one of the larger jars.

Of course, it's common knowledge that Goblins eat other Goblins, but not like this. There's always ceremony involved. Intimacy.

As he chews, the Goblin's eyes seep with tears.

And the General says, "I give myself few allowances when it comes to pride, but I do deem myself excellent judge of character. And I have no doubts that you, Escapist, will soon become one of our finest soldiers. Suffice it to say, I'm pleased you decided to stay with us."

"Thank you," I say, as the arm bone snaps. "Sir."

After the training session, I brew a pot of root tea and try not to think about home. And like usual, I fail.

Swan sips from his cup, and says, "I can taste your misery."

"I'm sorry, sir," I say.

The soldier shakes his head. "No need for apologies. I only wonder if there's something I can do to lift your spirits."

"I doubt that, sir."

"Well. If you ever need a friend, don't hesitate to call on me."

"Thank you, sir."

Swan drinks for a while, then readjusts his already straight hat. "I'm not supposed to tell anyone this, but you could use some good news." He leans forward a little. "General says he's not a Gnome who lets himself hope for the best, but due to recent developments, he believes the tide of the war will soon change. Very soon. He doesn't want the whole Army to know, so don't tell anyone else."

"Why would he want to keep this quiet?"

"General says his solders have lost enough already. He doesn't want to build up their hope and then crush it again, if he fails."

"If he feels that way, then why did he tell you?"

Swan looks as if I insulted his dead fathers. "I'm his best friend."

"Of course." I drink some tea, and I taste my bitterness. "Do you know what he's planning?"

"Not exactly. But I have an inkling it has to do with Number Twelve. We found that Gob dead this morning, and I never saw the General so happy. Like a youngling seeing a Fairy for the first time."

"I see."

And I try to remember the first time I saw a Fairy, but that part of my life seems too far away.

I'm a soldier now. A conjurer-in-training.

A Gnome without a name.

Jeremy C. Shipp

Instead of visiting the nightworld, I follow myself west. Toward the Farm.

I try to silence my mind, quiet my demons, because they keep telling me to turn back. They're not trying to protect me, of course. They just want the Goblins to suffer, for killing Feather Thundersoul.

For creating me.

More than once, I almost lose myself in the moonlit dark. But finally, I reach the Line, where the Forest ends, and the Farm begins.

My legs give way, as the looming fortress presses against my spirit.

I can't move.

And the figure before me removes his hat, his Gnomehood.

He reaches deep in the cloth.

"Feather!" I say. "Stop!"

To my surprise, the Gnome who turns around isn't me at all.

It's General Torrent.

And suddenly, I remember why I'm here.

"Don't do this, sir," I say.

The General grins, and says, "Don't save our kinfolk from mass murder?"

"Yeah."

"And why not?"

"Because this isn't right."

"Right?" The General laughs. "War is never right, Escapist. You of all people should understand that."

I stand on shaky legs. "Swan told me what the Goblins did to your Love, sir. I know you want revenge, but this is too much."

"I appreciate your empathy. However, I am not the Gnome you think me to be. My actions are borne from compassion for our people."

"Don't give me that, General. I know how much you hate the enemy, because our hearts are the same. There's a reason you kept Number Twelve in the same hut as your laboratory."

"I was utilizing space."

"You wanted him to watch as you created the disease that would annihilate his kind. You took pleasure in his torment."

General Torrent sighs. "I only want to save our world, child. Surely you must see the good in that."

"What if the disease spreads to other creatures?"

"That won't happen. My greatest thinker developed the illness with me. The Flower Curse can be carried by any mammalian, but Drum assures me that only Goblins will be affected."

"Drum is a Thundersoul, sir. She's a creative woman, but the Gnomes of my clan have a difficult time foreseeing the full spectrum of consequences of our actions. I'm sure she doesn't want to believe that the disease she created could kill all of Gnomekind, and so she won't let herself believe."

"I appreciate your concern, but I assure you. I've thought this through. There is no other way."

At this point, I realize the General's had this entire conversation with himself already.

He hid his plan from the Army, because he knows there are soldiers who'd try to stop him.

He knows the disease could spread.

He knows all the Gnomes and beings of the Forest could die.

And maybe, deep down, he doesn't care.

Before I can say another word, General Torrent pulls a mouse out of his hat, and tosses her on the ground.

I run.

I catch the mouse.

And the General says, "You know I won't let you take her."

"I know," I say.

"If you really want to stand by your convictions, you'll have to kill me. Otherwise, I stop at nothing to release the plague."

My whole body trembles. "I don't want to hurt you."

"Of course you don't. And my heart breaks at the thought of harming you. But this is war. Perhaps now you understand what that means."

"Promise me that you'll abandon your plan, and I'll let you go."

The General chuckles. "You're not going to defeat me, child. You're not the hero we pretend you are. You escaped the Farm on a fluke."

"I know. But I can't let you do this."

"Well then. Are you ready?"

"No." I set my hat on the earth, and place the mouse inside. Then I place a stone on the opening to keep the creature trapped inside.

"Are you ready now?"

I shake my head. I feel like I'm back at the Farm, naked and alone.

The General races toward me.

And we fight.

I see smears of blood, blurry faces. Sometimes I'm the General. Sometimes I'm the soldier.

Nothing makes sense anymore.

Maybe I'm saving my own people from possible extinction.

But more than that, I'm saving the Goblins.

I'm becoming the enemy.

My inner demons scream at me, and tell me there's still time to end this madness. To beg for forgiveness. To stop thinking so much about what's right.

But I can't stop.

I won't.

And while I'm no warrior, I do know something about causing pain.

I learned from the best.

So I do to the General what was done to me. And my spirit's back in my cage. Curled up on the floor. Begging for mercy.

But I show none.

"I'm sorry," I say.

And soon, the General stops struggling.

I didn't think I was capable of murdering one of my own kind, but maybe torture can do that to a person.

Maybe my compassion can only be expressed as cruelty.

After a bout of vomiting, I dig a hole to bury the General. I dig so deep that I almost can't climb out.

"Goodbye, sir," I say, and start walking away from the grave.

Then I remember the mouse.

I retrieve my hat, and lift the creature by the tail.

If I released her anywhere near the Farm, the Goblins would eat her, or they'd consume what consumed her. And they'd get infected and die. And since Goblins leave their dead out to rot, the flowers on their skin would blossom, and the pollen would spread. And that would mean the end.

So I need to remove this mouse from the food cycle.

I could kill her, of course. Dispose of her body so that no mammalian could eat her.

But the thought makes me vomit again.

I'll return to the hutment, and burn Number Twelve's corpse before the flowers have time to bloom. But then I'm done being a soldier.

I'm done with this war.

I still don't want to go home, so I'll journey south instead. I'll face the dangers of the Forest, and I'll protect this mouse to my last breath. I'll take her to the Fairies, and they won't let anything eat her, and she'll live the life I can't.

Obviously, they'll have to destroy her, if she starts flowering. But at least I can give her a chance.

And as I hold this small creature close to my heart, I feel like Feather Thundersoul again.

And the sensation only lasts a moment.

But that's long enough.

Ula Morales

I may look like your ordinary 10-year-old girl with antlers, but I'm actually rather special. I'm a Guardian of the Forest, and my mom was a very wise, very angry tree named Oak Mother.

She was a beautiful tree, especially in her old age, and her roots stretched all over the world. Into buildings, into people. Even into ideas.

For a while, my mom tried her hand at being a superhero. She used her roots to suck the life out of corrupt politicians, and rapists, and serial killers. But she soon discovered that the more evil she destroyed, the more evil she created.

And so, she realized that only a human could solve the human problem.

That's why my mother stole some hair from an old dying woman named Ula Morales. And that's how I got my name and most of my DNA.

Still, I am who I am today not because of my genetics, but because of my real mother.

Mother Oak was the one who loved me. Sheltered me. Fed me.

I was a hungry baby.

Every day, Mother Oak imbued every drop of sap I swallowed with love and loathing and knowledge and power. I devoured mind after mind of scientist and kung fu master and revolutionary, and I always wanted more.

Eventually, my mother gave me everything she had to give.

And as the last of her spirit leaked from her body, she said, "Promise me that you'll leave this forest. Promise me that you'll save the world."

So I stood tall, and said, "I promise."

In other words, I lied.

And she died.

She died, never knowing that she failed to create a savior.

Sure, I'm haunted by an unbearable desire to save the world, but even more than that, I'm afraid of leaving my forest.

I'm a coward.

Don't get me wrong. I'm not afraid of humans. What I fear is humanity.

I fear losing myself in their jingles and distractions. Their prejudices. Their rationalizations. I may be stronger than every other human on this planet, but I'm still one of them.

I'm still a frightened little girl, desperate for love.

But I shouldn't complain too much. I have a few friends in the forest.

My best friend's name is Never the Moss Fairy. The only problem with our relationship is that we can't stand each other.

For instance, yesterday in my tree hut, I spent two hours fuming about overfishing, and Never responded by saying, "I don't believe in oceans."

"How can you not believe in oceans?" I said.

"I've never seen any oceans."

"You've never seen oxygen either. Do you believe in oxygen?"

"Not really."

Our conversations always end in a brawl, and my physical strength can't compare to a Moss Fairy's magick, so I always walk away with scrapes and bruises and burnt hair. As for Never, he can't feel physical pain, so I try to hurt him in other ways. I tease him. Call him names. He usually ends up crying his eyes out.

But it's not all blood and tears. We do get along when we're sleeping. Never makes an excellent pillow, and I make an excellent nightmare-slayer. Sleeping so close together, our dreams often coalesce. So I protect Never from the flame beasts whenever I can.

During my waking hours, I'm usually alone.

Most of the forest animals avoid me because they fear me, and most of the forest spirits avoid me because I'm too depressing.

Sometimes, at night, Never travels to the homes of grieving parents and he leeches from them the memories of their dead children. Then, he gives me these memories to play with.

I get along well with these children, probably because they're not alive. But they don't last long. Memories never do.

Sometimes I fantasize about meeting another child like me in the forest. A girl with antlers. A girl who knows more about the world than she should. A girl who needs me as much as I need her.

But this fantasy girl never enters my forest. Instead, I get hunters like this one. And instead of embracing a kindred spirit, I have to fight an enemy.

So I fall from the sky and block the man's path.

"You look younger than I expected," the man says.

"I am younger than you expected," I say. "I'm ten years old."

He laughs. "A ten-year-old god. Right."

"I'm just a little girl."

He points his weapon at my face. "Then this should be easy."

"If you don't leave right now, I'm going to have to kill you."

That's not true exactly. I could let him live, but I'm no god. I'm a twisted child who wants to destroy this man, because I need someone to blame.

After the kill, I toss the hunter as far as I can. I don't want him becoming part of my forest. Part of me.

On the way back to my tree hut, I cry for the hunter's daughter. I imagine her with my face, and when she learns of her father's death, she screams with all her power, and the whole world shatters.

Eventually, my tears dry, and Never climbs into my hut.

"I found you a magic circle," he says.

"It's a CD."

"It doesn't smell like a seed."

"CD. Compact disc. You go to the human world all the time. How can you not know what this is?" Of course, I already know the answer to that question. Never is a master at ignoring anything and everything that doesn't interest him.

"Are you going to thank me for the present or aren't you?"

"Thank you."

"Goodbye."

"Wait. Where did you find this?"

"In your mom's rotting corpse."

"Why would you say that, Never?"

"Because it's true."

"Oh."

Never leaves me alone with the CD, and I can smell my mother. For some reason, she kept this human object inside her. I need to know why.

So I touch the CD to my heart, and I listen.

And while the strange sounds ravage my mind's ear, I connect with the soul of every human who ever listened to this object. And unlike most of the humans I deal with, these souls see me for who I really am. And they fear me.

I suppose these humans are the reason my mother decided to spread out her roots and touch the world. She felt sorry for these people.

Of course, I feel sorry for them too.

I just can't let that stop me.

I've never connected with anyone before, spirit to spirit. And I can't pass up this opportunity.

So I press the CD close to my heart, and I saturate the souls with my mother's sap, and I listen to them scream.

I don't empty myself completely.

Just enough.

Of course, I have no idea what these people will do with the love and the loathing and the knowledge and the power I've given them.

But at this point, I don't really care.

Spider House

I tell Roan that I'm heading to the supermarket for some peanut butter cup ice cream, but instead, I will myself to the barrens where I summon skeletons and command them to act out my past.

And so they do.

Years ago, during the real battles with real human beings, I would hide in my tent and drink tea. I would let my subconscious self handle the magic that protected my soldiers. And I would distract my conscious self with music or books.

Now, I watch the battles take place. Of course, during these reenactments, everyone's already dead. But I force myself to imagine their flesh and blood.

And eventually, among faces of the dead, I see my father.

That's when I decide to go home.

Back in Spider House, I spend some alone time in my room. Crying, manifesting old photographs, burning them again. Then I make Roan a new face, using the Snoopy carving kit Evening bought for me for my birthday.

I cut out the eyes, the nose, and a cruel part of me wants to cut out a frown. Maybe I want to hurt Roan's feelings. Or maybe I want him to yell at me for once. Burn me. Punish me.

Of course, Roan would never do that.

And, of course, I cut out a big, stupid grin.

Downstairs, I transfer the fire sprite from his old droopy Jack-o'-lantern, to the new one. Then I hold Roan in front of the bathroom mirror.

"I'm gorgeous!" Roan says. "Thank you!"

"I'm glad you're happy."

"Me too! I love being happy. Are you happy?"

"Not really."

"Oh no...." His voice breaks with emotion. "I'm so sorry, Shanna."

"Don't worry about it."

"Do you want to sing together?"

"Not right now."

"Can you carry me to Evening? I want him to give me compliments."

"Where is Evening?"

"He said he was going into the online dimension to find information about love."

"I see. I'm afraid I can't enter the online world the way he can, so we'll have to wait for him to come back."

"How long will he be gone?"

"Not long. Do you want me to turn on your cartoons for you?"

"Yes! I like cartoons. Do you like cartoons?"

"No."

"Oh no...."

"I'm gonna cook dinner now, OK?"

"OK. I like dinner."

Jeremy C. Shipp

Evening's not the demonic spirit he used to be. A year ago, he would scream at the top of his ethereal lungs, lacerate my skin with his claws, gnaw on my spirit with his fangs.

Tonight, he sits on the side of my bed and says, "May I?"

And of course, I nod.

I wouldn't be able to sleep at night without Evening sucking out my energy.

With a smile, the demon places his hand on mine. "Thank you."

I don't feel his touch, but my body begins to relax.

Evening glows.

"Tell me a story," I say.

"Alright," Evening says, and stares out the window at the night. "Once upon a time, there was a wild, happy boy who loved his parents with all his heart. They were good parents. They taught him how to make baskets and they told him they loved him all the time. One evil day, a group of soldiers came to the boy's village. The villagers tried to fight the soldiers, but the soldiers were protected by an angel of death. Then the soldiers blew up my parents, and chunks of them flew everywhere. One of the pieces even flew into my mouth. I was so sad and angry and dizzy. The soldiers pointed their weapons at me, and I really didn't want to die. But I didn't want to live either. Then time froze, and a man funneled out of my heart. He looked a lot like my father, only he was taller and he didn't wear glasses. He offered me a spiky seed and he didn't say a word. But he didn't have to. Somehow, I knew everything. I knew he was me. The me who could have been, but never would be, because of those fucking soldiers!"

The room rumbles, and my clock falls off my wall.

"Sorry," he says. "So then, I ate the seed."

And every time Evening tells this story about how he lost his heart, he seems that much closer to finding it again.

Barely awake, I say, "You're not falling in love with me, are you?"

"No," he says.

"Who is she then?"

"He. He's a shrub spirit from Connecticut. He's very nice."

"I'm glad."

It seems General Thomas Reed is still the man he used to be. He barges into my house, unannounced, and serves himself a large bowl of my curry.

"Thanks," he says, and sits at the table.

"What are you doing here?" I say.

He sips the curry like soup. "This is good. Did you make this? I mean, from scratch?"

"Yes."

He squints at the Jack-o'-lantern on the table, and laughs. "Don't tell me this is the same stupid sprite you kept as a pet during your tour. What's the point in keeping it burning?"

"He's not a pet."

"Sprites are just tools, Shanna. They're barely alive."

"Get out of my house."

He grins. "I missed our little arguments."

"I'm serious, Thomas. Get out."

He drinks up some more curry.

"Are you sad, Shanna?" Roan says.

"Yes," I say.

"Oh no...."

And at this point, Evening funnels out of the computer.

"We have a guest?" the demon says.

"No," I say.

"Is this man bothering you?"

And part of me wants to say, "Yes. This is the man who ordered the attack on your village."

And part of me wants to watch all the love in Evening's heart transform into hate. And I want to see the General's smirk falter when Evening attacks.

Of course, Evening might not recover from another episode.

And, of course, I say, "I'm fine. I just need to talk to this guy alone for a while."

"Are you sure?" Evening says.

"Yes."

So the demon returns to my computer, to his shrub spirit.

Before Thomas can take another sip of curry, I turn the bowl to dust.

"You're leaving now," I say.

The General sighs. "Listen, I didn't come here to fight with you. I need your help. Your country needs your help."

"I don't care."

"Things are bad out there, Shanna. The werewolves and the vampires are interbreeding. The aliens formed an alliance with our own androids. Even the trees are against us."

Part of me wants to believe him. I want to forget everything Evening taught me about war, and I want to become the angel of death once again. Because, the sick truth is, some twisted part of me believes that if I kill enough people, I'll eventually feel more powerful than my father.

And then, maybe, I'll be able to move on.

But I'm stronger than I used to be. So I say, "Your sales pitch isn't gonna work on me this time, Thomas. I know we can't solve all our problems with war. I also know you don't give a shit about solving our problems. You just want to benefit from them."

The General chuckles. "Amazing what you cowards tell yourselves to help you sleep at night."

"Fine. I'm a coward. Now will you please leave me alone?"

"Yeah. For now."

And he grabs a handful of my grapes, and walks away.

I sit at the table, take a deep breath, listen to the spidersong in the air.

"Are you sad, Shanna?" Roan says.

"Yes and no," I say.

"I'm sad."

"Why?"

"The man said I'm a sprite. But I'm not a sprite. I'm a gorgeous pumpkin."

"You are a sprite, Roan. There's nothing wrong with that."

"Sprites are tools."

I touch the side of the Jack-o'-lantern, and looks into its eyes. "I'm sorry that I haven't been a better friend to you, Roan. You've helped me so much, and I guess part of me feels embarrassed about that because you're a sprite. But that part of me is prejudiced and stupid and wrong. You deserve to know how much you mean to me. And...well, the truth is, you're the heart of Spider House. I'm sure Evening would agree with me on that. Sometimes, your kindness is the only thing that gets me out of bed in the morning. And...I can't imagine my life without you."

"You like me?"

"Yes, Roan. I like you."

Monkey Boy and the Monsters

Or Not To Wash

Monkey Boy threw his poo into the toilet—to be a good monkey, while at the same time acting upon his animal instincts. His nose traced circles in the air as he watched his dark mass descend into the Abyss.

Then, of course, he washed his hands with Soapy. "How ya doing?"

Soapy waited for Monkey Boy to finish rubbing him before he spoke. "Not so good, Monkey Boy."

"Why?" He dried his hands.

"Just been thinking. You know, about life."

Monkey Boy nodded—pretending to care.

Soapy paced back and forth on his soap dish. "Life is a strange thing. I get rubbed, massaged, every day of my life. And it feels really, really good, you know? But...but I can't ignore the fact that eventually I'll be massaged into nothingness. How can something that feels so good be the cause of something so bad?"

Monkey Boy shrugged.

Soapy stopped walking and looked at Monkey Boy in the face. "And so I'm really only left with two options, aren't I? One, live a happy, soapy life—and die. Or two, live a stale, lackluster life—and live forever."

Monkey Boy snapped out of the trance of soap-induced boredom he was frozen in. "Uh...interesting thought. But we gotta go, Soapy. You ready for the war today?"

"Yeah. I'm ready."

Georgian

Monkey Boy fought on two fronts. One was, obviously, the physical war out there, and the other was the mental combat that occurred in here. Here being the home of Bill, Renee, and Tommy Robinson—the General, the Prostitute, and the Georgian.

Tommy sat, hands over face, with tears in his eyes—like usual.

Monkey Boy jumped on the child's bed and petted him. He liked Tommy, because Tommy wasn't afraid of his pain. (The General and the Prostitute, however, were afraid of their own shadow selves. The General didn't lead an army into battle—instead, he forced Tommy to clean his room twice a day, and made Renee line up the silverware at the table just right. The Prostitute didn't sell herself for money—instead, she did everything everyone asked of her, because she couldn't stand the idea of not being liked.)

"You should just tell 'em, Tommy."

"I know. I know that's what I'm supposed to do. Parents are supposed to love their kids no matter what. But I know it's not going to happen that way. They won't love me as much anymore if I tell them. Do you know how I know that?"

"How?"

"Because when I first realized that I was Georgian, I didn't like myself as much anymore. Mom and Dad hate Georgians, and so part of me hates Georgians too. Which means, in some twisted way, I hate myself."

Monkey Boy monkey-laughed. "You liar. You go out with other Georgians almost every night. You told me you're having the time of your life."

"I am, but—"

"No buts. Let me ask you something. Do you really believe Georgians are any different from other people? Deep down, I mean. Deep down where all the poo is."

"No."

"Well then you shouldn't be afraid. Bill and Renee might be shocked at first...they might even be mad...but just give 'em a little time. They'll come around. They love you, Tommy."

"Yeah. You're right." He sighed. "I'm just so scared."

Monkey Boy smiled.

Pixie Dust

Faeries were just as mean and bloodthirsty and dastardly as any of the monsters (and perhaps even more so), but since they were cute and small (and no one could really understand what they were saying), the humans let them hang around.

Monkey Boy, nested in a chandelier, kept an eye on the dinner party down below. The owner of the mansion had hired Monkey Boy to make sure things went smoothly. He swatted at a few faeries who buzzed a little too close to his nose. They stunk like burning tires. They also, according to the humans, brought "atmosphere" to parties by throwing "magic pixie dust" on the guests. Which was really just a mixture of vomit, urine, and feces.

A man in a top hat stood. "Hello all, and welcome to the annual Family Wholesomeness Conference. As you all know, we are here to decide what is wholesome and what is not. Children everywhere are depending on us, so let us act cautiously and in an all around snooty manner."

"Here here!"

"First on my list—the word booby."

At the mention of the word, many of the men giggled like Japanese schoolgirls.

"Now then, the word booby has many meanings. It is a type of bird. It may also be used to propose that someone is ignorant. But—lately—when people say booby, they are usually referring to the female breast, which of course is a horrid, horrid thing for any healthy family to talk or think about. I propose—"

The door of the mansion exploded, and zombies flooded the room—moaning, hissing, growling, and making other stereotypically monster-like sounds. No matter how many times attacks like these occurred, people never learned. Sometimes, when a person wished too hard for a dead loved one to come back, it happened. They always came back as mindless, flesh-eating corpses, but that didn't seem to matter. People didn't change. They didn't care about the consequences of their thoughts—their dreams. Even if the whole world became swamped with zombies, people wouldn't stop tossing their pennies into wells or wishing upon disintegrating meteors.

Monkey Boy went to work. He threw poo balls at the eyes of the creatures (and blinded many of them) before leaping off the chandelier. The Conference people were so caught up in their discussions, they didn't seem to notice what was going on. Even when the zombies started gnawing on and devouring their flesh. Monkey Boy jumped from body to body, slashing, biting. He didn't hate zombies, so he had to use the trick his old fighting instructor, George, informed him about. George had fought in Nam, so he knew what he was talking about. George said that in order to kill something you don't hate, you should imagine that thing as something you do. So Monkey Boy didn't see zombies—but people. Poachers, specifically. Poachers brought back to life so Monkey Boy could get his revenge. He didn't think the poachers were bad people—they were probably nice enough guys out trying to make enough money to feed their families—he just hated them. Hatred had nothing to do with how good or how bad a person was—just what the people did. And these poachers had killed Monkey Boy's family.

The reanimated bodies had been decaying for a long time, so it didn't take much clawing before the chest cavity erupted and spewed out rotting organs.

Cleanliness

Monkey Boy sat on the floor, gasping for air. This had been one heck of a fight, and it had produced one heck of a mess. Blood, guts, everywhere. And if there was one thing rich, powerful people like these didn't like, it was filth. After their meeting was over, the first thing they'd notice would be the eyeballs on the table—not the cuts on their arms or the massive gashes on the backs of their necks.

That was where Soapy came in. Monkey Boy reached in his pocket and set the little talking cube on the floor. "All yours."

Soapy nodded (the best a soap could nod) and started licking. He dragged himself around and left a trail of sparkle in his wake.

Monkey Boy was sure glad Soapy had a thing for human flesh.

He sometimes wondered—but not too much, because he liked getting paid—why the rich people didn't leave raw meat outside the door, like most people did to keep the zombies at bay.

After a few thoughts ping-ponged in his skull, he decided they just really, really, really, really didn't like solicitors.

Hair in Strange Places

There came a point in human history when the void of poetic justice grew so large, irony itself anthropomorphized. Werewolves. Zombies were nothing compared to the werewolves. At least zombies wouldn't put an acid tablet into a businessman's wallet so the next time he wore it, the tablet would break, and burn a hole in his pocket—and his flesh. Zombies would never use laughing gas on clowns, or test cosmetics on corporate scientists, or gut fishermen. They wouldn't steal a woman's breast milk and feed it to a baby cow, or a woman's egg and feed it to a chicken.

Monkey Boy, an expert in werewolfism, was often hired by parents to check on their children.

Today he sat on a glass table—and gobbled up the fresh batch of cookies the mother just finished baking.

Fungus of the Heart

"Would you like anything else, Monkey Boy? Soda? Tea?"

"Got any bananas?"

"No. I'm so sorry! I should have—"

"I'm just kidding, Mrs. Stevens." He grinned. "I have a few questions for you before I go in there."

"Go ahead."

Monkey Boy scratched the top of his head. "You said Samantha's been acting different lately. How exactly?"

"Well, she's really sarcastic sometimes. She laughs at things I don't think are funny. And she stays in her room a lot."

"I see your point. I'll go talk to her."

"You won't hurt her?"

"Not unless you pay me to." Monkey Boy released a barrage of high-pitched chuckles and hopped off.

He leapt upstairs and entered the girl's room without knocking.

The girl was on her bed, listening to music. She removed her headphones. "You...you're Monkey Boy."

Monkey Boy nodded and jumped beside her. He pointed a finger at her. "If you try to eat me, I swear I'll slash your arteries."

"I won't."

Monkey Boy sat and drummed his fingers. "Your mom says you've been acting kinda poopy lately."

"Kinda poopy?"

"You know what I mean. Sarcastic. Secretive. The whole bit."

"Yeah, so what."

"So what!" Monkey Boy hopped up and down on the bed, screeching gibberish. After a few moments, he managed to calm himself and sat again. "I don't want you to become my enemy, Samantha. This is a war, you know. People are dying every day."

"I know." She looked down at her feet. "I don't feel right anymore."

Monkey Boy put a hand on her leg. "It's a scary time, I know.

You just gotta control yourself. Make sure you don't cross the line, ya know?"

"I feel like I can't control it. I look at myself in the mirror, and I don't see me anymore. I see a werewolf. Monkey Boy, I—I'm starting to grow hair in really strange places."

"That's not something you should be afraid of. It doesn't mean you're necessarily going to turn into a werewolf."

"It doesn't?"

"No. Even your parents have hair in strange places."

"I didn't know that."

"Well now you do. Do you feel better?"

"Yeah."

"I'm not going to have to come back and break your head open, am I?"

"No."

Monkey Boy nodded. "Good. Now I don't want to leave here today and have your mom call me tomorrow and ask me to come back. Before I go, tell me, do you have any substances in here?"

"No." Her eyes darted away for a split second.

"You don't mind if I look around then?"

"Course not."

Monkey Boy bounced off the bed and rummaged through her drawers, crawled under the bed, and when he approached her closet—

"Don't!"

Monkey Boy turned around. "What? What do ya have in there?"

"Just things. Personal things. I don't want you to see."

"I already went through your underwear drawer. How much more personal could it be?" He flung open the door. And there it was. A penguin dressed in a tuxedo. Sick, sick irony. "No substances, huh?"

"That's uh—that's my pet."

"Sure it is." He grabbed the penguin and tossed it out the window. He'd call animal control later. "I don't like when people lie to me."

"I don't like when monkeys get all in my business!"

Monkey Boy stared at her.

Samantha broke into tears. "I'm sorry. I didn't mean...." She wiped her cheeks. "I want to stop. I really do. It's just so hard."

"I tried compassion. I tried being a good little monkey. Didn't do any good. There's really only one other way I can think of to get that sarcasm off the tip of your tongue." He reached in his pocket and pulled out the white hunk. "Wash your mouth out with Soapy."

Romanticism

Vampires—the worst of all.

They emerged in many forms—mostly boy bands and idol singers. More than anything, vampires feared death. They were obsessed with the idea of being lost in the Abyss. And so they spent their entire lives attempting to become immortal.

To accomplish this, they sucked out the essence of society's youth. They took children's souls and replaced them with song. Romanticized fluff. "If you believe in yourself, you can do anything." "Love is great." "Oh girl." "Oh boy." Blah, blah, blah. All they were doing was setting up kids to be destroyed in the real world.

Another reason he despised them—there were no Georgian vampires. Not marketable enough.

Monkey Boy hated the soul-suckers and he took every chance he got to rid the world of the bastards.

There they were. In the bus.

Monkey Boy paid the taxi driver, climbed out the window, and leapt into the open window of the vampires' vehicle.

The vampires within screamed and waved their hands about like little girls.

Monkey Boy rushed at them with wooden steaks. T-bones, of course.

They attempted to render Monkey Boy unconscious by singing one of their horrible songs, but Monkey Boy had remembered his earplugs.

"You greedy, greedy monsters." Monkey Boy stabbed another one. "You don't care about what you're doing. You don't care that your immortality has a cost." He kicked one in the groin, and ducked, avoiding a punch. "Doctors, scientist, philosophers. They'll all be forgotten. But you don't give a damn. It's all about you, you, you!" He finished the last one off.

Soapy climbed out of his pocket and looked at the mess. "Should I?"

Monkey boy shook his head.

"Why?"

"No matter how many of these bastards I kill, more and more of 'em keep popping up. We'll dump 'em in the middle of town. Word of warning, so to speak."

Image

During dinner, Monkey Boy "accidentally" knocked another plate onto the floor. He liked to watch the General's face as his perfect little Universe became a chaotic, jagged jumble—even if it was just for a few moments.

The General had to laugh it off, of course. Seeing as the money Monkey Boy brought in made up about ninety-nine percent of the household income.

Renee gave him more mashed potatoes. "So how was your day, Monkey Boy?"

"Same-o, same-o."

"What about you, Soapy?"

"We cleaned up." Soapy smirked.

Tommy cleared his throat. "I uh—I have something to tell everybody. It's not going to be easy for you to hear."

The General didn't look too happy.

Tommy continued. "I might as well just come out and say it." He took a deep breath. "I'm Georgian."

Silence devoured the room.

Fungus of the Heart

Monkey Boy didn't like quiet. He liked action. He liked people working things out—and as quickly as possible.

"So—" Monkey Boy wanted to say the words, but he was afraid. He was a public figure and if he said the three words, the world would find out. The world would look down on him, and then he might not get as many jobs, and then he wouldn't have as much money. But—

Monkey Boy sighed.

—but there were some things more important than what the world thought, and how much money he had.

Monkey Boy stood. "I'm Georgian too."

And that was the end of that.

Break From War

This was why he fought the war—why he allowed himself to do terrible, terrible things to terrible, terrible things. Sometimes Monkey Boy wondered if he was just as bad as the monsters he killed.

But when he was here, those thoughts drifted out of his head and disappeared—like spontaneously combusting butterflies.

It was the largest collection of paintings, statues, vases, and other forms of art in the world. And these weren't normal antiques either. They were famous. People spent years, decades, centuries admiring them. That was why it felt so good to mess them up. Every day, Monkey Boy smeared snot on works of art. Making the art of others, his. He chopped off the heads of Greek gods and replaced them with molds of his own. It was a power trip, but at least Monkey Boy wasn't afraid to admit it. He liked watching the expressions. People from all over the world came to visit Monkey Boy's special gallery. They would ooh and ahh, pretending that it didn't hurt their egos—pretending that it was okay that—during this time of war and suffering—humans would sacrifice art to the highest bidder. Even if it meant selling them to a primate who laughed at the idea of poo in the Mona Lisa's hair.

Monkey Boy sniffed his most recent acquisition, and decided it would be his new spittoon.

Dirty

Monkey Boy threw his poo into the toilet.

He washed his hands with Soapy. "How ya doing?"

Soapy waited for Monkey Boy to finish rubbing. "Not so good, Monkey Boy."

"Why?" He dried his hands.

"Just been thinking. You know, about life."

Monkey Boy gave a slight nod—faking interest.

Soapy paced back and forth on his soap dish. "The thing is...I'm the symbol of cleanliness, right? And yet, I come into contact with more dirt and goo and scum and grime and muck and glob and dust and—"

Monkey Boy yawned.

"—filth and puss and ooze and gunk and slime—than anything else in the world. Hell, I eat zombies for lunch. So what exactly does that make me, Monkey Boy?"

Monkey Boy shrugged.

Soapy stopped walking and looked at Monkey Boy in the eyes. "Am I, as a person, as an individual...really clean?"

Monkey Boy broke free from the spell of soapy snore-dom he was stuck in. "Uh...interesting thought. But we gotta go, Soapy. You ready for the war today?"

"Yeah. I'm ready."

Agape Walrus

There are four recognized subspecies of walri. The Pacific Walrus (Odobenus rosmarus divergens), the Atlantic Walrus (Odobenus rosmarus rosmarus), the Laptev Walrus (Odobenus rosmarus laptevi). And, of course, there's the rare Agape Walrus (Odobenus rosmarus kevinus).

One such walrus, Kevin L. Donihe, lives high up in the hills of East Tennessee. His diet consists primarily of sculpted tofu, because his best friend, Drippy the Zombie Polar Bear, wakes up every morning to shape the tofu into mollusks, tube worms, and sea cucumbers. Kevin appreciates the effort. So much so, that every morning, Kevin allows the bear to unlock and remove his titanium skullcap. Then, Drippy uses a sterile X-Acto knife to cut a miniscule chunk out of Kevin's head.

Kevin eats the tofu. Drippy eats the brains.

And this is what scientists like to call a symbiotic relationship.

Scientists use words like symbiotic, because they don't understand love.

That's why Kevin invites a sampling of scientists to his tree house for a feast of the heart. And out of the twenty scientists he invites, only seven RSVP. And out of that seven, only three end up attending.

Doctor Bloss (marine biologist), Doctor Ivanova (ethologist) and Mr. Wire (time-travelling cytologist).

But before the guests arrive, Drippy says, "Maybe I should leave."

"Don't be ridiculous," Kevin says.

"I'm not. I just...I'm not like you, Kevin. I don't have anything to offer humans. Or anyone, really."

"Don't say that. You're such a syrupy-sweet soul, with a huge heart of glimmery gold. I just want to gobble you up like a bowl of lemongrass curry."

Drippy smiles, a little. "What if they've never smelled a zombie before? Won't my scent makes them throw up everywhere?"

"Don't worry, Drip-drop. Humans are visual-based creatures, usually. Just drench yourself with cologne, and their senile sniffers will be none the wiser."

"Well...if they are visual beings, then what if I'm the first zombie they've ever seen? What if the sight of me makes them faint?"

"Undead Americans are all the rage in the human world. Everyone sees them in magazines and movies."

"But those zombies are airbrushed and reconstructed with plastic surgery. I'm hideous!"

Kevin slaps the bear's back with his flipper. Affectionately. "You're my lovely little lily. You're my pretty peachy princess."

"Stop."

"You're my darling doll. My stunning star. My gorgeous gourd."

Drippy can't help but grin.

"Will you stay for the party?" Kevin says.

The bear searches through his treasure chest for his bottle of Chanel No. 5. "I'll stay."

So, hours later, Drippy presents the humans with a platter of tofu burgers, tofu fries, and tofu apple tofu pie.

"You have a beautiful home," Doctor Ivanova says, wrinkly and smiley and small as a child. "I love the colors. The curves. Are you, by any chance, a fan of Antoni Gaudí?"

"Who?" Kevin says, sucking a tofu burger off his Elves Presley limited edition collector plate.

"I don't mean to be rude," Mr. Wire says. "But this food tastes like shit."

"I um…" Drippy says. Then he sniffles, and charges into the tofu preparation room.

"My festering friend in a sensitive soul," Kevin says. "You'd best keep your criticisms to yourself, Mr. Wire."

The grimy cytologist shrugs. "I'm sorry."

But he doesn't sound sorry.

And Kevin can't help but grin. He loves a challenge.

Doctor Ivanova glowers at Mr. Wire. And when she frowns, her whole crinkly face joins in. "If you will excuse me, gentlemen." She rushes into the kitchen, and licks Drippy's festering wound.

Kevin spends the next few minutes chatting with Doctor Bloss about the weather.

But eventually, the ethologist returns to her cement clam of a chair.

And Kevin says, "A feast of the heart has little to do with physical sustenance, so we'd best get down to those brassy tacks." He faces the marine biologist. "Tell me why you're here, Doc. Tell me why you think you're here."

"Well," Doctor Bloss says, running his hand through his ashen hair. "I'm here to study you. I would love to remain in the area for a few days and monitor you in your natural habitat. If it's no problem for you."

"I'll give it a think." He faces the ethologist. "And what about you, Doc? Why are you here?"

"Well," Doctor Ivanova says. "I wanted to meet you. And I wanted to observe the social interactions between an Agape Walrus and a Zombie Polar Bear. Your relationship is quite fascinating."

Kevin nods, and faces the cytologist. "And you, Mr. Wire? What do you want from me?"

"Absolutely nothing," Mr. Wire says. "I'm here to collect a sample of zombie cells from the bear."

"I see," Kevin says. "Now, do you want me to tell you the real reason why you're all here?"

Fungus of the Heart

The three scientists stare at the walrus.

Doctor Ivanova looks amused.

Doctor Bloss looks confused.

And Mr. Wire looks bored.

"You're here for love," Kevin says. "Who wants to go first?"

After a few moments, Doctor Ivanova raises her hand.

Kevin smiles. "Hippity hop on over here and take my tusks."

The ethologist obeys.

"Now press your face against my whiskers, if you would be so kind."

The ethologist obeys again.

"This might tickle a bit," Kevin says.

And as his tusks turn the color of a Gold Lamé Suit, his glowing whiskers wriggle and writhe their way into the doctor's face.

"What the fuck?" Doctor Bloss says.

Entering the doctor's heart, Kevin expects to find a malnourished spirit in need of a savior. But instead of confronting his stereotype of a scientist's soul, he finds himself wrestling a whirlwind of sunshine and smiles and silly stories.

The force of the doctor's love knocks the breath right out of him.

Her love is pure. Her love is true. And even more shocking to the walrus, her love might just be purer and truer than his own.

Kevin sighs. Sure, the doctor's love causes him to burst with ecstasy, but still, he feels somewhat disappointed. And more than a little jealous.

Finally, the one soul splits into two.

"Thank you," Doctor Ivanova says, collapsing to the flowery floor.

Kevin looks at the two men. "Who's next?"

Doctor Bloss wipes his face with a lacy handkerchief.

"Doctor Bloss?" Kevin says.

"I wasn't raising my hand," the biologist says.

At this point, Drippy returns to the feasting room, and nuzzles his snout against Doctor Ivanova's nose.

"Doctor Bloss," Kevin says. "If you connect with me, I'll let you stay here for a week. I'll let you watch me eat and sleep and jig. I'll even weewee and poopoo in front of you."

The biologist bites at his fingernail.

"You have nothing to worry about," Doctor Ivanova says, wrapped up in the arms of the bear.

"What do you say, Doc?" Kevin says.

Doctor Bloss closes his eyes, nods.

"That's the spirit!" Kevin slaps the biologist's back with his flipper. Tenderly.

And moments later, Kevin finds what he expects to find in the doctor's heart. He finds an emaciated spirit, no more than skin and bones. The soul clings to Kevin. The soul gazes at him with puppy dog eyes.

And the man and the walrus become one.

Kevin drowns Doctor Bloss in a tidal wave of crabs and colors and the King's Christmas album.

After the separation, Doctor Bloss collapses to his knees, with snot and tears oozing down his blushing face. He wraps his beefy arms around the walrus. "I wanted to kill you." He sniffles. "I wanted to kill you and the bear. I'm sorry, Mr. Donihe." He hugs Kevin tighter. "I'm not Doctor Bloss. I'm a fucking poacher. Why am I a fucking poacher?" He presses his face into Kevin's blubber and sobs, hard.

"I forgive you," the walrus says.

The poacher collapses, and crawls on hands and knees over to Drippy.

Then, Kevin turns to Mr. Wire. "If Drippy gives you a bit of blood, will you let me love you?"

The smelly cytologist shrugs. "Fine."

"You're not gonna clone me, are you?" Drippy says. "Because I don't really believe in cloning."

"Clone you?" Mr. Wire laughs through clenched teeth. "I'm looking to wipe all you bastards off the face of the Earth."

Fungus of the Heart

"Why would you do that? I mean, genocide is wrong."

"That's the point, you idiot. Decades from now, zombies will mutate into mindless killing machines. And my mission is to find a way to prevent the apocalypse."

"Oh...well..." Drippy scratches at a boil with his claw. "Alright then."

"That's settled," Kevin says. "Now let's get all lovey-dovey, shall we?"

Mr. Wire shrugs and connects with the walrus.

And Kevin supposes that inside Mr. Wire's heart, he'll discover a rotting carcass of a soul in desperate need of resurrection.

Instead, Kevin encountered an abyss. And not just any abyss.

This abyss is pure. This abyss is true.

Kevin stares at the void with his mouth wide open. And he feels himself drifting closer and closer to the nothingness. And part of him knows that he needs to snap out of this state of shock, so he thinks about Drippy's rumbly chuckle.

And the walrus and the man disconnect.

Kevin finds Drippy by his side, crying, growling his name.

"I'm alright," Kevin says.

"You were screaming," Drippy says. "And I wanted to separate you two, but you said...you told me I should never do that, no matter what. Are you OK?"

"I'm peaches and cream. But I can't say the same for Mr. Wire. He has a big boo-boo in his ticker."

"What kind of boo-boo?"

At this point, Mr. Wire sticks a sparkling syringe into Drippy's open wound. "Thanks for the blood, asshole."

"What's wrong with your soul?" Kevin says.

"What's wrong with your soul?" Mr. Wire repeats, in a cartoonish voice.

Then, the cytologist studies the syringe in his hand. He chuckles, and tosses the zombie blood out the open shark-shaped window.

"Why would you do that?" Drippy says.

Mr. Wire shrugs.

Kevin looks into the man's eyes, hoping to find some answers.

But before Kevin can figure anything out, the god of life and death whispers the secret into Drippy's heart.

As a zombie, Drippy's privy to all sorts of fascinating facts.

"Mr. Wire doesn't have a soul," Drippy says. "Only the physical body can travel back in time. So he...you know...left his soul back in the future."

Mr. Wire snorts. "Ridiculous."

Ridiculous, yes, but Kevin trusts his friend.

And so there's only one thing Kevin can do for this soulless monster.

"I want to love you," Kevin says. "One more time."

"I don't need your love," Mr. Wire says.

"Pretty please."

The sunburned cytologist shakes his head.

So Kevin blocks the front door. "Hold him down, Drip."

"What?" the bear says.

"Hold him down."

"But you said before we should never force people to share their soul with you."

"He's not a person, Drip. He's a big bad boogieman, and he needs my help."

"I guess you're right."

And so, Drippy holds down Mr. Wire, while Kevin gives him a piece of his soul.

It's not much, of course.

But it's enough.

Later, Mr. Wire stares at himself in the bathroom mirror. He runs his crusty finger up and down the frayed edges of his tattered silver jumpsuit.

Then, he takes a long, hot bath.

And as for Doctor Ivanova and the poacher, they're spooning on the linoleum.

"Should we wake them?" Drippy says.

"Not yet," Kevin says. "Let's let them feel all fuzzy-wuzzy for a while longer."

The bear nods.

And all through the night, Kevin dreams of the abyss.

And when he wakes, the nightmares refuse to end. He fears the nothingness will haunt him forever.

So after Drippy sculpts the morning tofu, Kevin allows the bear to unlock and remove his titanium skull. Then, Drippy uses a sterile X-Acto knife to cut out a miniscule chunk of memory out of Kevin's head.

Kevin eats the tofu. Drippy eats the brains.

And this is what some scientists like to call love.

Kingdom Come

My Filter edits out the utility wires and pollution, so I can truly appreciate the view. And as foggy fingers caress the curves of the earth, I think of heaven. Not the heaven I envision today, with walls and guns and sentinels. No, I'm reminded of my childhood heaven, where everyone wears flip-flips and walks on clouds.

I was a stupid kid.

And in my undeveloped mind, I imagined my parents and my sisters and me living together in a white castle, one big happy family again. I knew this would never happen in my lifetime. But I thought if God embraced my father, forgave him, then my mother would follow suit.

Back then, I didn't know much about my father. Sure, I knew he was a coward. I knew he refused to fight. And I knew he was the worst kind of man, because that's what my mother told me. But I thought I loved him anyway.

I loved him, even when my mother cried and told me she couldn't go on. And I tried to convince her life was worth living. I talked about her favorite foods, and my good grades, and Christmas.

After my rambling, she would hug me and say, "You're a brave boy. If you were older, you'd fight for me. I know you would."

And she was right.

But the war's over now, and I'm sitting on top of the world, or at least at the highest overlook in Kingdom Come Park and Penitentiary.

The Cumberland Plateau bursts with fall foliage, dazzling my eyes.

I feel so small. So connected.

And as I read in the brochure, these feelings, they're a warning sign. Symptoms. If I don't medicate myself soon, I could develop a full-blown case of Thoreau Syndrome.

So I hop off the stone column, and lead my family to the Art Hut.

There, I sit on a bench and study the black bears.

And I chuckle, cured of the reverence plaguing my soul. These creatures look so pathetic, stuffed in glass boxes like the contortionist I once marveled at in my youth. But unlike the performer, these creatures inspire only pity, victims of their own weakness.

Sure, beasts like these posses a certain raw strength, but their power can't compare to that of a human being. Of an American.

Therefore, these bears will live the rest of their wretched lives in these boxes, with tubes jammed in their orifices and flesh.

I laugh again.

Then my son cries.

And I notice a young couple. Pointing, smiling.

"What's wrong with you?" I say, holding my son's shoulders.

"They want to go home," he says.

"Who?"

"The teddies. Can't we let them go with their mommies?"

"Stop crying."

And after I touch my belt, my son obeys.

"Maybe I should take him outside," my wife says.

"No," I say. "He needs to see this."

An older man in a suit steps closer to me. "It's refreshing to see a father taking an interest in his son's artistic development. You'd be surprised what a rarity that is these days."

"You're right. I am surprised."

The old man grins. "I'm John Miller, the Curator."

"Samson Carter."

We shake hands.

And after a few minutes of talking about black bears, we shake hands again.

"See you tomorrow night, Mr. Carter," the Curator says. "Assuming you and the missus are planning on attending the show."

"Show?" I say.

"I'm surprised you haven't heard. All of Kingdom Come's buzzing about tomorrow's guest. He's supposedly quite the comedian."

"I doubt we'll be in attendance. I'm not a comedy fan."

"Well, to each his own."

Outside the hut, my son approaches one of the glowing rhododendrons, and I have to grab him by the arm.

"Don't touch those," I say. "Don't even get near them."

"Why?" my son says.

"Because I told you not to."

And that's the end of that.

One good thing about my son, he knows when to shut up.

Thankfully, my Filter's sophisticated enough to differentiate between the day-to-day screaming in Kingdom Come and the yelling of my wife. So the machine lets me hear her, and I wake up.

And I find her on her knees, a few meters from the tent.

"What's wrong?" I say.

"It took our son," my wife says. "It took our son."

I glance around. I don't see him. "Who took him?"

"A monster." She cries.

I feel like shaking the truth out of her, but there's no time for that. "Which way did they go?"

"I don't know. It pushed me into a bush, and when I got up, they were gone."

By now, a small group's formed around us, and a middle-aged woman steps forward. "I seen what happened. They went that way." She points.

"Call the Guardians," I say, and look down at my wife. "Don't tell them what you think you saw. They'll lock you up."

"Your wife ain't touched," the middle-aged woman says. "I seen the creature too. I can corroborate her story."

But I trust this hick even less than my wife.

"Tell them you can't remember," I say to my wife.

She nods.

And I run.

A few times, I stumble on steps and the roots bulging from the earth, and I remember the veins that swelled on my mother's forehead whenever she exercised or threw my father's porcelain horses at the wall. She limited herself to only destroying a couple every few weeks, because she wanted them to last.

Eventually, I end up catching my breath beside what looks like a fallen petrified tree. But no, I read about this in the brochure. Log Rock's a natural sandstone bridge, and my Filter's supposed to edit out all the vandalism, the names and messages scratched into the stone.

For a few moments, however, I see enormous letters that run almost the entire length of the bridge.

THE MONSTER IS INSIDE.

And I hear a chorus of screams.

Then, silence.

I follow the escort into the Coal Mining Museum and Guardian Headquarters, up the stairs, to a large office on the fourth floor.

Standing in front of Warden Rose is almost like looking in a mirror. The same buzz cut. The same color suit. And if you squinted, you might mistake one tie for the other.

While the escort whispers into the Warden's ear, I let my eyes explore the photographs on the wall. Photographs that the Warden obviously acquired from the exhibits, because the pictures impart a bloody history of the coal industry. Mining accidents, burning houses, dead families. I also see some newer photos of the reconstruction, when the mines were transformed into the jail it is today.

Warden Rose shakes my hand, smiles. "Do you always bring suits along on your camping trips, Mr. Carter?"

"Yes," I say.

He sits, and motions for me to do the same.

I obey.

Then he leans forward, frowning. "I want you to know, we're making every effort to find your son. We already tracked down his Filter, but I'm afraid the device wasn't attached to his head."

My head vibrates with a shiver. "Would such a removal cause him any permanent damage?"

"That depends on our enemy's knowledge of Filters, and the tools at his disposal. For now, let's assume your son is alive and well."

I nod. "Do you have any leads?"

"Yes. But I didn't call you here to brief you on the investigation. Your desire to assist in this case is understandable. However, you aren't qualified—"

"I fought in the war, Warden Rose. I'm more than capable of—"

"With all due respect, Mr. Carter, your attempts to help would only reduce your son's chances of survival. I read your file, and I know you're a man of myriad abilities. But this is a matter of harmony. If I allowed you to enter our system, we could no longer synchronize and achieve perfection. I hope you understand, I'm not trying to insult you. I only want to save your son."

I still feel angry, but I also feel more respect for this man and his organization. "I understand."

"Good. Now." The warden taps a button on his desk, and a monitor lowers from the ceiling. "As you must know, there are security cameras in place throughout Kingdom Come. One such camera captured the initial moments of the kidnapping." He presses another moment.

And I see a monster with black matted fur and metallic fangs. It pushes my wife's chest. Snatches up my son. Runs.

Then the warden turns off the monitor. "I don't blame you for not believing your wife. Like me, you're a man who refuses to accept outlandish stories without empirical data."

A hint of guilt tingles in my gut, but the feeling's soon overpowered by rage. I told my wife not to talk about the monster, and she did so anyway.

"But now you've seen the truth," the warden says. "Now you can give your wife the validation she needs. Don't tell her about the recording. Just tell her you believe her. And convince her that what she saw was a man in a suit. I'm sure she'll see reason, if it's coming from you."

I nod.

"One more bit of advice," Warden Rose says. "Take your wife to the show tonight. I hear our guest is a genius in his field."

"I'm not in the mood for comedy," I say.

"That's exactly why you should attend. Laughter is the best medicine, Mr. Carter. At least promise me that you'll consider the matter further."

"Alright."

"Good." The Warden stands, and I do the same. "I'll contact you as soon as I find your son."

"Thank you."

We shake hands.

And halfway to the door, I turn around. I almost forgot. "My Filter's been malfunctioning ever since my son was taken."

The Warden sits. "How so?"

"The audio and visual editor shut off once, for a few seconds. And my dialectal translator doesn't seem to be working at all anymore."

Warden Rose rubs his eyes. "I apologize for the inconvenience. To be honest, the Filters have a hell of a time coping with the effects of heartbreak. Still, this is no excuse. My Guardians assured me they'd stomped all the bugs in this new model, and they're going to suffer for their failure, I assure you. I'll send a technician to your tent tonight, and he'll fix your Filter while you sleep."

"Thank you," I say.

And all the way back to my tent, I search myself for the heartbreak warden Rose spoke of.

Sure, I find annoyance, outrage.

But I don't feel any sorrow.

In fact, I can't even picture my son's face.

The Guardian tries to stand, fails.

So I help him to his feet. "What happened?"

"I'm sorry, sir," he says. "It ate my gun, knocked me unconscious. I'm sorry."

I check the tent.

Empty.

And still, I don't feel anything but anger.

Anger at the monster, of course.

Anger at this pathetic excuse for a Guardian.

And more than that, anger at myself. Because what kind of man doesn't protect his own family?

A man like my father, that's who.

I punch my forehead, hard.

Fungus of the Heart

And a few hours later, I'm lost among the trees. This isn't easy to accomplish, due to my impeccable sense of direction. But I manage, somehow.

Once again, the natural world makes me feel small, connected.

Calm.

And I realize, I'm not even looking for my wife and son anymore.

Because without my fury, I'm numb.

Empty.

Or maybe not.

Maybe the words on Log Rock were meant for me.

Maybe there's a monster inside me.

I laugh at the thought, and then feel an aggressive desire to return to my tent.

But I ignore the emotion.

Eventually, I find myself staring at a patch of thirty two luminescent flowers, and part of me hopes that my Filter will malfunction again.

Then my wish comes true.

And there are thirty two men and women sitting on blackened circles of earth, weeping, screaming, the hairs on their bodies sticking straight out.

They look ridiculous.

I search their faces, looking for my father.

He was caught four years ago, so there's a chance he's serving his time here.

I used to tell myself that I didn't want to confront my father, but right now I feel eager, desperate.

And I don't know if I want to hug him or kill him.

Probably the latter.

But I don't find out, because he's not one of the men.

As I sit there, watching them shake and jerk in agony, I begin to feel a faint cramp in my chest.

Empathy.

I feel sorry for these insurrectionary bastards, when I can't even muster the same sentiment for my own missing family.

There must be something truly wrong with me.

"You deserve this," I whisper.

These people are political prisoners of the worst kind. And if the Guardians didn't force these traitors onto the anomalies, the unhampered energy would erupt and find another human body to bind with. Man, woman, or child.

The energy doesn't discriminate.

So if someone has to suffer, better the guilty than the innocent.

Better them than me.

According to Warden Rose, criminals are like coal. If you press them hard enough, they'll eventually become diamonds. But once in a great while, the Guardians find themselves clashing with an unfortunate soul beyond help, beyond hope.

Hunter Hill is one such devil.

"I can't give you back your family," the warden says. "But I can give you Hunter."

So about thirty minutes later, I'm underground, in a white room, holding the warden's gift, tight.

Hunter struggles against the ropes.

Useless.

I let out a primal roar, and judging by Hunter's expression, I'm a monster in his altered vision.

A monster with black matted fur and metallic fangs.

Just like the warden promised.

"Beg," I say. "Beg for your life."

Hunter trembles. "I ain't playin' your games no more, Rose."

"I'm not the warden."

"Whoever. Just do what you come to do, and let me back in my cage."

"You're not going anywhere until you beg."

"No."

I growl and slash his face with my claw.

"Fuck you, Rose," Hunter says.

"My name is Samson Carter," I say.

"Don't ring no bells."

"You killed my family." I take the gun out of my pocket.

And how this looks to Hunter, I don't know. Maybe I'm ripping the weapon out of my flesh.

"I knew you was Rose," Hunter says.

"Will you stop saying that?" I say. "I'm Samson Carter."

"You got the warden's gun."

"He let me borrow it."

"Nah, you wouldn't never let anybody touch your pistol."

After a deep breath, I point the gun at his face. "You killed my family, and now you're going to die."

"I ain't no killer. That's why I got sent here in the first place."

"Shut up." I cock the hammer.

A tear rolls down the bastard's cheek, and he closes his eyes. "Goodbye, Earl."

I lower the gun. "Who's Earl?"

"I weren't talkin' to you."

Again, I point the gun between his eyes. "Who's Earl?"

"A better man than you."

And I consider pressing the matter further, because I see love and respect for this man swarming in Hunter's eyes. And if this Earl is a prisoner in this facility, maybe I could torture him in front of Hunter.

The warden would probably permit me that right.

But I'm feeling more than a little tired.

So I pull the trigger.

And Hunter's skull bursts with fall colors, dazzling my eyes.

I laugh.

Then metallic fangs gnaw on my innards, and I double over and vomit.

I've killed men like Hunter many times before.

But somehow, this feels different.

I feel different.

And maybe the warden was wrong about me.

Maybe I'm not brokenhearted.

Maybe I'm just broken.

I try to stand, fail.

The audience laughs.

I'm in a cave, and Guardians fill the amphitheater risers, and Warden Rose approaches me, smiling.

"What am I doing here?" I say.

"You're here for the show," the warden says. "You're going to entertain us with your comedy."

"What?"

Warden Rose helps me to my feet, then points his pistol at my face. "Get on your knees."

I obey.

"Beg for mercy," he says.

"Why are you—"

"Beg!"

"Please. Don't shoot me."

"You can do better than that."

Fungus of the Heart

I force my hands together. "Don't shoot me!"

The Guardians laugh.

Warden Rose lowers his weapon, and smirks. "You're pathetic. You know that, don't you?"

I don't move a muscle.

"I asked you a question, Earl," the warden says, looking right at me.

"What?" I say.

"I said you know you're pathetic, don't you, Earl?"

I don't know why he's calling me that, but I nod anyway. "Yes."

"Good. Now we can start the second act." He presses a button on a remote.

And my mind surges with fear, and I imagine my body filled with TNT.

But, of course, I don't explode.

Instead, my Filter hums and drops off the back of my head.

"I have some questions for you," the warden says. "They should be easy enough for an intelligent young man such as yourself. Are you ready?"

"Yes," I say, because he's still holding the gun.

"Who are you?"

"Samson Carter."

"Wrong." And he shoots my leg.

I collapse, screaming.

The audience cheers.

"Let's try that again." The warden points his gun at my other leg. "What's your name?"

But I don't answer, consumed by my hatred for this man.

"Hurry now," the warden says. "Before your time runs out. What's your name?"

"Earl," I say.

The warden nods. "Now tell me the names of your wife and son."

I grasp at shadows. "I don't know."

And in fact, I don't think I ever knew.

"One last question, Earl," the warden says. "What's your last name?"

I open my mouth to say, "Carter."

Then the fog clears.

And I know myself again.

"Hill," I say.

That's the right answer, but he shoots my leg anyway.

Just like I knowed he would.

"Enough questions." The bastard points at a space behind me. "Let's begin act three."

I look back.

And John Miller, the Curator, winks at me, standin' beside a small glass box.

"Fuck you, Miller," I say, and turn back. "Fuck you, Rose."

Rose chuckles, then flicks his hand. "Put him in."

I struggle against his foot soldiers.

Useless.

So they get to work.

And I think about what they done to me.

Raped my mind with their fuckin' machine.

Made me act like 'em.

Think like 'em.

Even tricked me into killin' the man I love.

I shake and jerk with sorrow.

And when they're done with me, I'm naked, trapped in a much smaller cage than I'm used to, tubes jammed in my holes and flesh.

Rose faces his men.

Gives a big thumbs up.

Applause, applause, applause.

Fungus of the Heart

I thought I knowed every nook and cranny in these fuckin' mines, but this here room is new. And I thought Angelica was dead, but there's her rabbit tattoo on the squashed body in front of me. I reckon there's at least a hundred men and women boxed up in here, stacked on a giant circle of black stone.

And I know Rose wants to keep us here for the rest of our lives.

Because we're troublemakers, the whole lot of us.

Unfortunate souls deemed beyond help, beyond hope.

I added my name to Rose's shit list the day I escaped the mines. I knowed I wouldn't get far, of course, but I wanted a victory. Even a small one.

And after I broke out, I had just enough time to write on that log. THE MONSTER IS INSIDE.

I reckon Rose thinks I'm referrin' to him in that message, callin' him a monster for all the fucked up stuff he's done.

But that ain't it.

The monster's inside me. Inside all us captives.

Rose and his men don't know that, of course. They don't know nothing about the monster and the so-called anomalies.

They don't know the anguish we feel with this energy gushin' inside.

They don't know how eventually, if we remain in this state long enough, we transcend the pain.

And when that happens, a monster transcends the earth.

And fills us.

Sure, the beast don't have black matted fur and metallic fangs.

But she's dangerous.

And as her electric fingers caress the curves of my tormented body, trying to work her way inside me, I think about my childhood hell. With walls and guns and sentinels. Even then, I knowed hell was a prison built to keep certain folks out of heaven.

I was a smart kid.

And in my hopeful mind, I imagined myself breakin' my mama out of hell, and takin' her to a cabin in the woods, where we could live in peace.

Back then, my mama was the world to me. Even after she died.

Sure, I knowed she was a traitor. I knowed she defied the will of the government. And I knowed she was the worst kind of woman, because that's what my foster parents told me. But that only made me love her more.

I loved her, and when I growed older, I did everything I could to honor her memory.

So when my government demanded that I fight in their war, I refused.

They throwed me in prison, and I'm sure they reckon I'm a coward. But what they don't understand is that I'm a warrior at heart.

And one day, the Monster, she'll grow strong enough to free us from these cages.

And then the War will finally begin.

How to Make a Clown

The blurry clown in my attic looks a little like my father, and maybe that's why I hear him out. Maybe that's why I don't smash the walnut wall mirror where he resides. Or maybe I'm just lonely.

"Where'd you get that scar?" I say, pointing to the puff of pink under his left eye.

And the clown says, "I crashed my moped into a forklift."

"Just like my dad."

The clown chortles. "What a coincidence."

"Tell me again why you're here?"

And he does.

And for the next hour, day, week, month, the clown tries to convince me to cross the threshold into the mirror.

He tells me he needs me. His world needs me.

Ordinarily, I shy away from sober conversations like this. I don't even talk politics with my co-workers. But the guy in the mirror is a clown, and I can't for the life of me take him too seriously. In fact, most of the time, I'm laughing on the inside.

For the sake of my sanity, I pretend that I'm completely and utterly shocked by this whole situation. Sometimes, when I'm alone on the toilet or the loveseat, I look at the ceiling and I whisper, "What the hell is going on up there?"

But, to be honest, my life has never made more sense to me.

Fungus of the Heart

Ever since I locked eyes on the mirror at that old fighter pilot's yard sale, I knew where my life was headed, the way someone takes one look at a stranger and thinks, "This is the love of my life." Or the way a child realizes, for the first time, "I'm going to die someday."

So every morning, I climb the stairs into the attic. And every morning, the clown lies to me.

"You're the chosen one," he says.

"You have a destiny," he says.

He says, "Without you, my world will be torn in two."

And while I know I'm nothing special, I do enjoy the fantasy. So I spend my days feeding my aching body with DiGiorno pizza, feeding my aching heart with cheesy romance novels, and feeding my aching ego with the mirror.

On my birthday, the clown blesses me with a particularly beautiful lie.

He says, "You're stronger than you think you are, Fergus. Stronger than your father."

"What do you know about my father?" I say.

"Not much. But I know he was a coward."

"Well. If you can call a war hero a coward."

"I can."

And so, it's out of gratitude that I say, "I'll do it. I'll save your world."

The clown wipes his sweaty forehead with a violet handkerchief. He laughs. He smiles his second smile. He says, "My hero."

And before I can change my mind, I press my trembling hands against the mirror and I tumble into the world beyond.

My wonderland reminds me of my mother's favorite painting. I don't see any weeping willows or weeping schoolgirls here, but I feel lost and happy and alone, the way I imagine my mother felt when she stared, smiling at the work of art in the hallway.

As a child, I always wanted to ask my mother what she saw beyond the paint. But of course I never did.

I didn't want to taint her happiness with my involvement. My existence.

About two weeks before my mother passed away, I almost asked her for the painting. But instead, I held her hand and said, "I'll never forget you."

And she said, "I'm sorry."

Now, I pretend that my mother can hear me, and maybe she can. I say, "At least you never beat me."

Hours later, I'm wandering the onyx ruins, searching for water, when a giant scarab charges me.

So I do my best impression of my father, and kick the beetle in the face.

The scarab twitches. Then stops twitching.

And a tiny man in a violet tunic charges me with a knife.

The spirit of my father leaves my body, and I collapse, trembling, myself again. I say, "Please don't hurt me."

"Why did you kill her?" the man says, his blade pointed at my stomach.

"I didn't want to die."

The man drops the knife. He cries. He says, "She was harmless."

"I'm sorry."

"Mary was my friend."

"I'm so sorry." I look the stranger in the eye for the first time and I think, "This is the love of my life." I think, "I'm going to die someday."

So I'd better start living.

Part of me doesn't want to taint this man's sorrow with my involvement, but I hug him anyway. I say, "I'm sorry." Again and again.

Finally, he says, "It was an accident," and he wipes his face with a violet handkerchief.

"Do you know any clowns?" I say.

Fungus of the Heart

"What? Why?"

"Never mind."

Two weeks after we meet, Moore forgives me for killing Mary by leaving a blood rose under my pillow. The first thing I do is smell the rose and forgive my mother. Then, I walk the five miles to my soul tree, and I dig a hole with my hands, and I bury the rose.

Months later, I'm in our honeymoon tent, crying.

"What's wrong?" Moore says, and kisses away my tears.

"Your family doesn't like me," I say.

"My sweet giant. You need to stop mistaking love for loathing."

"They do loathe me."

Moore rubs my back. "They don't."

Minutes later, Moore's father, Aiden, enters the tent carrying a gift wrapped in mauve bear fur. I know it's a gift because of the water rose on top.

Aiden kisses me between the eyes. He takes my hands. He says, "You're a good man, Fergus. Good for my son, and good for the tribe. I would love for you to stay with us until time's end."

"I'd love to," I say.

The old man grins, unwraps the gift, and hands me a semi-antique hand-carved walnut wall mirror.

After the honeymoon, I spend an entire morning sitting under my soul tree with a sun rose in my hands, gathering my courage.

Finally, I ask Moore for his knife.

"Are you sure about this?" Moore says.

I want to say, "I don't mind making a fool of myself for love," but Moore doesn't really get my humor yet. So I keep the bad joke to myself.

"I'm sure," I say.

And right as the blade touches my face, my soulmate says, "The image in a mirror is reverse."

"Right."

So I cut myself under my right eye instead.

After the blood dries, Moore paints my wound with yellow clay.

"Why don't you just tell him the truth?" Moore says. "Tell him his true love is waiting for him on the other side."

I shake my head. "If I said that, he'd break the mirror."

"Why?"

"He'd want to punish me for my cruelty. Love is the one thing he wants most in the world, and love is the one thing he knows he'll never have."

"But that's not true."

"It doesn't matter. He'd never believe the truth, so I'll have to tempt him with lies."

"I don't understand him, Fergus."

"Me neither."

I wake up with a grin, because today's the day. The day the other Fergus will cross the threshold.

At least that's what I'm thinking until Moore hands me a wind rose. A rose of parting.

"In case we never see each other again," he says.

"What do you mean?" I say. "We know he'll come here, because I came here. Right?"

"He might come here. Or he might destroy the mirror and kill the man you've become. Today he'll make the choice, and I'm afraid the choice is his alone."

"That's not fair."

"I know."

"I don't want to die. I don't want to lose you."

He kisses my tears. "My sweet giant."

"I can't do this. Will you talk to him for me?"

"I would if I could, but in the reflection of the mirror, I can only see the man I used to be."

"What happens if I lose you?"

"Then you'll grow old and you'll find me in the next life."

"I can't live without you."

"You can. You're stronger than you think you are, Fergus. Stronger than your father."

And maybe he's right.

So I face the mirror one last time, and hope for a hero.

About the Author

Jeremy C. Shipp is the Bram Stoker nominated author of *Cursed*, *Vacation*, and *Sheep and Wolves*. His shorter tales have appeared or are forthcoming in over 50 publications, the likes of *Cemetery Dance*, *Apex Magazine*, *ChiZine*, *The Magazine of Bizarro Fiction* and *Withersin*. Jeremy enjoys living in Southern California in a moderately haunted Victorian farmhouse called Rose Cottage. He lives there with his wife, Lisa, a couple of pygmy tigers, and a legion of yard gnomes. The yard gnomes like him. The clowns in his attic—not so much. His online home is jeremycshipp.com.

Also by Jeremy C. Shipp

Cursed by Jeremy C. Shipp
hc 978-1-933293-86-8 • tpb 978-1-933293-87-5

Your life is no longer recognizable, corrupted by unknown forces. The harder you struggle, the more you suffer. That's because: a) someone or b) something is after you with a vengeance. That means you and everyone you know will: 1. suffer 2. die 3. amuse your tormentor. That is, unless you figure out how to manipulate the person behind this and turn their power against them.

"…a tightly written story of suspense and occult horror…" —*Publishers Weekly*

Sheep & Wolves by Jeremy C. Shipp
hc 978-1-933293-52-3 • tpb 978-1-933293-59-2

Jeremy Shipp is the master of the mind-bending tale. Much like his critically acclaimed novel, *Vacation*, these stories bewitch and transport the reader. Though you may not know where Shipp will travel next each story is an unforgettable thrill-ride and you'll be glad you took the trip.

"Any reader of the bizarro culture will find this collection a necessity, any reader of fiction will find *Sheep and Wolves* rewarding." —*Midwest Book Review*

Vacation by Jeremy C. Shipp
hc 978-1-933293-40-0 • tpb 978-1-933293-41-1

It's time for blueblood Bernard Johnson to leave his boring life behind and go on The Vacation, a year-long corporate sponsored odyssey. But instead of seeing the world, Bernard is captured by terrorists, becomes a key figure in secret drug wars, and, worse, doesn't once miss his secure American Dream.

"This is an intriguing, challenging, literate, provocative novel… — Piers Anthony

www.RawDogScreaming.com